HIS VOICE HOLDS ME in its tender spell. His eyes graze over my body without shyness—he takes me in as a landscape, a lush terrain of swells and valleys.

He leans forward, then. My heart thumps so strongly in my chest I am sure he must hear it. His face comes close, closer to mine—so close, a stray lock of his wild hair caresses my cheek.

I should move away. I do not. Instead, I close my eyes. My lips part and a sense of yearning fills me, a longing for something I cannot name. It is a force larger than myself that moves through me, ancient as the earth. There is no choice but to surrender.

Also by *Maryrose Wood:*

THE POISON DIARIES: NIGHTSHADE

THE POISON DIARIES

BY *Maryrose Wood*

BASED ON A CONCEPT BY
THE *Duchess of Northumberland*

BALZER + BRAY
An Imprint of HarperCollins*Publishers*

The Poison Diaries

Text copyright © 2010 by Poison Diaries Ltd.

www.epicreads.com

www.poisondiaries.com

Library of Congress Cataloging-in-Publication Data

Wood, Maryrose.

The poison diaries / by Maryrose Wood ; based on a concept by the Duchess of Northumberland. — 1st ed.

p. cm.

Summary: In late eighteenth-century Northumberland, England, sixteen-year-old Jessamine Luxton and the mysterious Weed uncover the horrible secrets of poisons growing in Thomas Luxton's apothecary garden.

ISBN 978-0-06-180238-6

[1. Human-plant relationships—Fiction. 2. Poisons—Fiction. 3. Medical care—Fiction. 4. Plants—Fiction. 5. Supernatural—Fiction. 6. Fathers and daughters—Fiction. 7. Northumberland (England)—History—18th century—Fiction. 8. Great Britain—History—George III, 1760–1820—Fiction.] I. Title.

PZ7.W8524Poi 2010   2009054427

[Fic]—dc22   CIP

                                                                                            AC

Typography by Charles Yuen

11 12 13 14 15   LP/BV   10 9 8 7 6 5 4 3 2 1

First paperback edition, 2011

For Jane
and her wonderful gardens

1

15th March

Gray skies; the rain came and went all morning. A cold wind blew in gusts, worsening as the day went on, until the lowest branch of the great chestnut tree in the courtyard splintered down the middle and crashed to the ground. If I had been standing underneath, I would have been crushed.

Spun wool after breakfast. Read for a short while, but my eyes ached too much from sewing to continue long. Changed the soaking water

for the belladonna seeds.

Father is still not home; it has been two days.

THE BERRIES OF THE BELLADONNA PLANT are beautiful. I have always thought so. I would string the plump black pearls on silk thread and wear them around my neck if they were not so deadly.

The seeds are nearly as poisonous as the berries; Father has warned me a thousand times. But I am careful. First I tie the seeds in clean muslin bags and drop them in a pail of cold water. Before they can be planted they must soak for at least two weeks, and I must change the water every day. That is how Mother Nature would do it: The snow would fall and melt and then fall again. And it would be too risky to leave the seeds in the ground during the cold months; they might get eaten by birds and carried away to grow in some distant field, where they could wreak their mischief without warning. Instead I make-believe a winter for them, to trick them into growing only when and where I wish.

2

Even after all that care, only a few seeds will sprout, and of those half will soon shrivel back into the dirt. Are you so in love with death, lovely lady? I call you lovely lady, for that is what "belladonna" means. You are curiously reluctant to be born. Is our world not beautiful enough for you? Or perhaps there is another, more perfect realm in which you prefer to dwell?

I laugh at myself now; what foolish imaginings! But when Father is away I must make do with whatever companions I can find: a sparrow on the windowsill, a shadow on the wall, or even a tiny, dangerous seed. We have lived alone here among the ruins for so long, Father and I, and he is away so much, and is so silent and lost in his own thoughts even when he is here, I sometimes worry I might lose my speaking voice completely from lack of use.

Let me test it.

"Hello."

"Hello?"

Feh! I sound a frog. A tincture of lemon balm and

anise would cure this broken voice of mine.

Or someone to talk to. That would do it, too.

I wonder where Father has gone, this time. Someone must be very ill to keep him away from home so long. Father is not a doctor, nor is he a "butcher" (that is what he calls the surgeons). But high born or low, when the people of Northumberland are sick, they send for Thomas Luxton. On the rare times when Father has let me go to market day and walk through the crowds, with my cloak pulled close around my face (he does not wish me to speak to anyone, for he says they will try to trick me into revealing secrets about his work), I hear the things they say:

"You're better off with Luxton than those university-trained doctors, with their ointments that blister the flesh, and their buckets to fill with your blood."

"Doctors! Tell 'em you've got a sore toe and they'll take a hacksaw to your leg!"

"Luxton may be an odd duck, but at least he doesn't burn you and bleed you and stick you all over with leeches.

4

Luxton follows the old ways, the lost ways. . . ."

". . . *the witches' ways*," some of them might add in a fearful whisper.

But Father would scorn the very notion of witch-craft. People call him an apothecary, but he considers himself a man of science, and a "humble gardener," as he likes to say. By that he means that he grows all the plants he needs to make his medicines right here, in the garden beds that surround our stone cottage. He grows other plants, too, in a separate walled garden behind a tall, black iron gate. The gate is held shut by a heavy chain, fastened with a lock that is bigger than my fist.

When I was small, Father warned me morning and evening never to approach the locked garden, until I was so afraid I couldn't sleep without dreaming of snakes chasing me. The snakes' bodies were links of thick metal chain, and their gaping jaws clicked open and shut like a lock, catching at my heels no matter how fast I ran. Finally I asked Father: "Why would anyone grow bad plants that have to be locked up behind walls? Why not only grow the good ones, and let the bad ones wither and die?"

"Plants are part of nature; they are neither good nor bad," he replied, drawing me to his knee. "It is the purpose we put them to that matters. The same plant that can sicken and kill an innocent girl like you can, if mixed in the right proportions, make a medicine that saves a young man from typhoid or cures a baby of the measles."

"But why do you keep some plants apart, then?" I demanded to know.

"Because of you, Jessamine. Because you are only a child. Until you are older, and have the wisdom to know what you may touch and taste and what you may not, I keep the most powerful plants behind the locked gate, where they cannot harm you."

"You don't have to lock the 'pothecary garden, Father." I pouted like the baby I was at the time. "If you tell me not to go in I surely will not."

"If you surely will not," he said with a smile, "then the existence of the lock should not trouble you in the slightest."

I have never won an argument with Father, but it is not for lack of trying.

I add more coal to the fire, and light a fresh candle to sew by. It is midafternoon, but the sky is thickly blanketed with clouds. The day feels dim as dusk.

Father must be working hard, wherever he is. I hope it is not a child who is ill. Not that I am squeamish about sick people. In fact, I prefer to go with Father when he pays his visits. I like to watch how men thrash about as they battle against terrible fevers, or how women moan and grunt as they labor to bring their babes forth, while Father mixes just the right medicines to help ease their pains.

But there is so much work to do at the cottage, especially with spring coming. Now that I am old enough to mind the house and care for the gardens myself, Father usually insists that I stay home.

So here I remain, with only my sewing basket and the wet seed babies of my lovely lady for company. A damp, shaded spot near the stone wall suits the belladonna plant best. Or so Father tells me. I have never seen it growing there myself, for I am still not permitted to enter the apothecary garden. It is too dangerous; I am too young, I do not know enough—Father is stubborn as stone and will not change his mind. Yet I want to learn. For now I content myself with leafing through Father's books and examining the specimens he brings home.

That is how I came to know the belladonna berries. Every autumn Father collects the lush, ink black fruits and preserves them in a glass jar, which he keeps on a high shelf in his study. In late winter he removes a few and delicately slits them open to harvest the seed.

This is the first year he has entrusted the seeds to me to prepare for planting. "Remember, Jessamine," Father warned, "you will be raising a litter of assassins."

That was Father's idea of a joke, but I knew to heed the warning. When I change the soaking water, I wear gloves and remember not to touch my fingers to my lips or eyes. After I finish, I wash my hands twice with lye soap and throw the gloves in a bucket of bleach. I place a lid over the pail that holds the seeds and the fresh water, tie it fast with strong twine, and mark it POISON.

I do this even when I am alone, as I am now— one never knows when a vagrant might wander by in search of a cool drink. Even those who cannot read will know the sign for poison. If they ignore it, they do so at their peril.

Then I carry the discarded soaking water far from the cottage and drain it into a swampy, overgrown ditch. I choose one so thickly surrounded by bramble and gorse bushes that the duke's sheep and cattle would never try to drink from it, nor any human, either.

Last week I found a dead cat by the ditch. But I think it had died of something else. Even so, when I told Father, he dug a hole and buried the body right away, and Father is no particular friend to cats.

It was a deep hole, deep enough for a man's grave. The cat was small, with soft orange fur. I know it was soft because I petted it to say good-bye, but the body was cold and stiff and Father told me not to touch.

I said a silent prayer, too, as Father shoveled the dirt back into the hole. Soon the last glimpse of orange had disappeared; a slight depression in the muddy earth was all that marked the place. Within a fortnight that would grow over with brambles, too.

"It is a rare beast that gets such a funeral," Father remarked, sweating and leaning on his spade. "Lucky cat."

Personally I think the cat would have been luckier had it lived. Then again, life for a stray, unwanted thing is not always pleasant, so perhaps Father was right after all.

And of course, we have other ways of keeping the mice away from our cottage.

Father laughs when I call Hulne Abbey "our cottage."

"It is a ruin, a wreck, a pile of weathered, moss-covered rocks," he always corrects me. But this is the only home I have ever known, and who can feel at home in a ruin? Anyway, Father exaggerates; where we live is no mere pile of rocks, though it is centuries old. It is not large, but it has a feeling of spaciousness; even, if you ask me, of grace.

That is no surprise. Father says our house used to be the chapel, in the long-ago days when the old monastery still stood on these lands. For miles around, the buildings and farms of the abbey stretched up through the hills until the distant spot where the planting fields end and the line of the forest begins. For five hundred years these fertile acres teemed with people and animals and life. No more, though. Now Father and I live in the chapel; the rest of the monastery is rubble, and all the Catholics are in Ireland and France.

Sometimes, when the weather is fair, I lie on my back in the grass of a nearby field. I close my eyes and try to imagine that last, terrible day, in the hours before it was all laid waste. But even the grandfather of the oldest person in the town of Alnwick was not alive to see it. There is no one who can tell me what it was like to hide at the edge of the forest, as I imagine

I would have done, watching in terror and fascination as the king's soldiers smashed the ancient buildings to bits and then hunted down the fleeing monks like so many helpless rabbits.

Father often says he wishes they had torn down the chapel and left the monk's library standing instead, but I like our home just as it is, a long, rectangular structure made of rough-hewn blocks of stone. Long ago Father divided the interior into rooms. My bedchamber is small and up a long flight of stairs, in the old bell tower. On the main floor is a bedchamber for Father, a study in which he does his work, and a front parlor where we take our meals. It is where I write my garden diary, too, at the end of each day's labors.

Of all these rooms, the parlor is the largest, and the one that still looks most like a church. There is a high, vaulted ceiling, and tall arched windows that Father says once had stained-glass pictures in them. Now they are filled with thick, plain glass that is divided into many small panes. On sunny days the light slants through the panes and makes narrow, glowing pathways across the dark wood planks of the floor.

I used to play hopscotch with those paths of light when I was small—*if I leap over the light without touching it, Mama will live*, I would say to myself. *But if my foot touches the light she will die.*

My foot never, ever touched the light—to this day I will swear it—but Mama died anyway.

Oh, how I wept! I was only four, so perhaps the outburst can be forgiven. But I remember how Father's voice stayed calm.

"That is the way of things," he explained to me at the time. "All creatures die when their time comes. No matter what we do, or how we may feel about it, nature always gets her prize in the end."

Father is always so strong and wise. Sometimes I wish I were more like him. I wish I could accept that the way fate has arranged things is both right and good, and that living here alone with him, sewing and cooking and tending the garden, and perhaps, when I am old enough—*perhaps*, in my mind I can hear him say it!—learning to help him with his work, as I am beginning to do now with the belladonna seeds, is exactly the way my life was intended to be.

But, other times, the scent of bread baking, a remembered, loving smile, or an especially lonely winter night, with no one to sing me to sleep, leaves me weeping in secret for Mama, and filled with a kind of fury I cannot name.

It happens less often as the years go by, though.

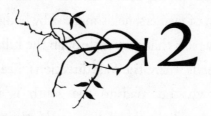

2

16th March

*The weather continues damp and cold; I built
a strong fire in the morning and still could not
get warm. Peeled potatoes and parsnips for soup.
Cleaned and oiled all the boots. Changed the soaking
water for the belladonna seeds.*

Still no word from Father.

FROM THE TOWER WINDOW in my bedchamber I
can see quite a distance: over the crumbling stone wall

that encloses the courtyard and cottage, past the quilt pattern of farmers' fields marked by hedgerows, to the narrow path that snakes through the hills to the main crossroads where the four directions meet.

Down the road to the south is the town of Alnwick, where the duke's castle stands guard over Northumberland. To the north, the Cheviot Hills and Scotland. The westbound road will carry travelers to Newcastle, if they are not murdered by highwaymen along the way. To the east lies the sea.

If I happen to be looking out of my window when Father returns, I will be able to see him coming two miles away, a lone, stoop-shouldered figure walking from the crossroads down the winding footpath that cuts across the sheep fields.

Even when the need for his services is urgent, Father prefers to walk. He likes to stop and examine whatever grows by the side of the road. There he might find a rare type of wildflower that he covets for our garden beds, or some creeping plant whose properties are unfamiliar to him, or a strange mushroom growing on the back of a rotted stump.

Many times he will return home from a journey with his satchel full of specimens. I always offer to sketch them for his plant notebooks. These notebooks fill many shelves in his study, but none of them contain the formulas for his medicines. That information is secret. The recipes for making his tinctures and tisanes, oils and ointments, smudge pots and poultices are recorded in a leather-bound volume he keeps in the locked bottom drawer of his desk. I have only seen it once, years ago, and then only because I walked in on him while he was writing in it—a mistake I have not made since—

I burst in without knocking and stood in the doorway to his study, a breathless, saucer-eyed girl with mud-spattered legs and a five-legged frog cupped in my hand.

"Look, Father! I found it in a puddle at the foot of the wall, that great stone wall that hides the 'pothecary garden! I ran straight back to show you. Have you ever seen such a freakish creature? Will it live? Should it live?"

As soon as he saw me he shoved the book away,

locked the drawer, and pocketed the key.

"Set it free, Jessamine." His eyes stayed fixed on his desk as if they would bore two holes in it. "The frog's destiny is no business of yours."

Now there are two men in the distance, but neither of them is Father. One is too short, and the other is too fat. They are the Wesleyan preachers, a loud-mouthed pair from one of the nonconformist sects. They used to come to the door now and then, in their long coats and strange hats, saying, "The end of the world is nigh!"

I find them funny, to be truthful. "The end of the world"—what a notion! As if there were anything to be done about that. Surely it would be better not to know.

I do not think the preachers will pay a call today, though. The last time they came, Father spoke to them very harshly. "That it will someday be the year eighteen hundred, rather than seventeen what-you-please, is a simple mathematical fact of the Gregorian calendar. It is a new century, not a harbinger of doom!" he bellowed. "Take your superstitions, and be gone!"

They have not knocked on our door since.

I watch through the window as the two figures disappear into the valley at the foot of one hill and reappear a short time later, as the path rises over the slope of the next. But there is no Father, not yet.

I awaken in Father's chair, the one in the parlor nearest the hearth. I had not meant to fall asleep, but an hour's sewing made me close my eyes to rest them. Now the cloud-veiled sun is low in the sky, and the skirt with the torn hem that I was in the midst of mending has slipped from my lap to the dirty floor.

Father is not home. Could some misfortune have befallen him? It makes my chest tighten to think of it, like a heavy rope has been coiled around my body and pulled hard, until I can barely breathe.

If something happened to Father, then I would truly be alone.

I would be alone with the cottage that once was a chapel, and the gardens, and the ruins, and whatever ghosts of dead monks still wander the fields. I might never have cause to speak aloud again.

Unless I left. I could leave, I suppose, if something happened to Father.

Why not? I could leave Hulne Abbey to crumble and the gardens to grow wild. Someday, after many seasons of snow and rain, the iron lock that seals the great black gate to the apothecary garden would rust and break open. The heavy chain would slip to the ground, and all the deadly plants would be loosed upon the world—

This is all more foolishness. I am used to being alone, and it is ridiculous to mind it. Father is fine, I know it. He is too clever and strong to let anything bad happen to him. And I have plenty of work to occupy me and keep my thoughts from straying into dark corners. I check my list:

I will turn over the empty garden beds and prepare them for planting.

I will spread a fresh layer of mulch over the strawberry patch.

I will cut back last year's dead growth on all the kitchen herbs, right to the ground, so the new sprouts will have sun and room to grow.

Good health to Father, I think nervously. *A quick recovery to his patient, whomever it may be. A safe and speedy return to the cottage.*

But it occurs to me: Perhaps there is no one sick. Perhaps Father is at Alnwick, at the castle library, lost in his research and the workings of his own mind, and that is why he has not thought to send word to me. Perhaps he has finally found the mysterious books he has sought for so long, among the duke's many ancient and dusty volumes—the ones he believes may have been rescued from the hospital of the old monastery, before the soldiers came to burn what would burn and smash the rest.

Do these volumes even exist? Father believes they do. He believes passionately and without proof, the way other men believe in God. He often talks of these books in the evenings in our parlor, a glass of absinthe and water in his hand. When he speaks of them, his speech quickens and his eyes flash.

"The monastery hospital was famous throughout Europe," he begins, as if I had not heard this tale from birth. "The monks' power to heal the sick was so great that the people called them miracle workers, and sometimes even saints." Then he laughs. "Anyone could be such a saint, if they had access to the same information as those long-dead holy men! Someone must have saved the volumes that contain all the monks' wisdom. It would have been madness not to."

He sips his green, licorice-scented drink and continues in this vein until the fire dies and my head nods forward on my chest.

Sometimes I think Father's hunger to know what the monks knew is a madness all its own. Once, long ago, I watched him dig up a ten-foot square in a distant field to twice the depth of his spade. He planted nothing, but visited the place daily for weeks, to see if

22

anything unusual had sprouted in the freshly turned earth.

"Did you think your shovel might wake the bones of all those dead monks, until they rise and tell you their secrets?" I joked nervously as I watched him sift through the dirt with his fingers.

"The monks may be dead, but their medicines still lie sleeping in the ground." There was an edge to his voice. "Hidden deep in the cold, dark earth, a seed can be nearly immortal. Even after so many years, if exposed once more to the light and air and rain, there is a chance some long-forgotten plant of great power may yet reveal itself."

I had meant only to tease, but instead I seem to have stirred Father's anger, for he kept muttering furiously to himself: "But what of it? Any discovery I make will be useless, unless I can learn the specimen's properties, its uses, its dangers. . . ."

"No one knows more about plants than you do, Father," I said, to calm him.

He climbed to his feet, dirt clinging to his knees.

All at once he was shouting. "Compared to the monks I know nothing! I dig blindly to rediscover what they took as common sense. The formulae all burned, the wisdom of centuries in ashes. . . . To kill such knowledge is itself murder—it is worse than murder—"

Father raged on. I stopped listening and let his voice turn to a wordless buzz, a hornet floating near my ear. All I could think was, *But how could a puny seed be immortal, when it was so easy for Mama to die?*

Wait, I hear someone at the door—it must be Father home at last—

3

17th March

Warmer today, but a steady wind blows from the east, smelling faintly of the sea. The sun peeked through the clouds briefly after lunch. Then gray skies once more.

Made breakfast for Father, who ate little and said less. After the meal he went straight to his study and locked the door. I am alone again.

Changed the soaking water for the belladonna seeds—only one more day before *they are ready for planting!*

Father still has not told me where he was.

I TRY TO BUSY MYSELF with chores. I practice sketching, though I can find nothing of interest to sketch: a kettle, a chair, a ball of yarn.

After lunch I can stand it no longer. The fire is still in embers, so I am quickly able to rekindle it and put on a kettle of water for tea. As soon as the tea is ready, I set it on a tray and proceed to Father's study.

Before I knock, I peer through the keyhole. What I see only fills me with more questions. Father paces around the room and mutters like a wild thing, grabbing volumes from the shelves and throwing them down again. His heavy leather-bound book of formulas, the one he keeps locked in a drawer, lies open on his desk. Now and then he comes back to the book and leafs through the pages, looking for something that he clearly cannot find.

I take a deep breath to calm myself and knock on the great wooden door.

"Father? I brought you some tea."

Silence. Then:

"I did not ask for tea, Jessamine."

"I want to speak to you."

A thud, as of a large book slammed shut. The bang of a drawer closing, the click of a lock. Father opens the door, the small gold key still in his hand.

"Speak, then. I am busy; I am sure you can deduce that from the state of my desk." He looks down at the tray. "What type of tea is it?"

"Lemon balm. Made with leaves that I saved from last summer and dried in the storeroom." I lift the tray higher, so he can catch the scent. "It is very soothing."

"Lemon balm tea," he echoes as I make my way past him and place the tray on his desk. The dark wood is pocked and crisscrossed with grooves from a few centuries' worth of scribbling pens. "Such a simple, harmless drink. Made by your own sweet hands, I presume?"

"Of course." I hand him the cup. Lemon-scented

27

steam rises between us. As he sips I gather my courage to ask, "Where were you, Father?"

"In my study, obviously. I have been in here all day."

"I mean yesterday. And the day before, and the day before that."

He turns away. "I was where my services were required; that is all you need to know."

"That is not an answer." I too can be stubborn—I am my father's daughter, after all. "I was left here alone for three days. Surely it is only fair that I know why."

He looks angry at first. Then his face softens.

"I am sorry if you were anxious, Jessamine. I was called away to deal with an urgent medical matter. It took up all of my attention; if you had asked me how many days I had been absent from home, I myself could not tell you."

"Called away to where?"

"I have been in London."

"London! Why? Where? Why did you not take me?"

28

He holds up a hand to stop my questions. "I have been places I hope you never go, and seen things I hope you never see. I was in London. That is all I will say, and even that is saying too much. Now forgive me; I must get back to work." He turns to retreat to his chair, then stops. "How are the gardens, Jessamine? Are you tending them well?"

"Of course. I have turned over all the beds, and planted the lettuce and radishes, and—"

He interrupts. "And the belladonna seeds?"

"I have changed the water every day, exactly as you showed me. Tomorrow they will be ready for planting." On a foolish impulse I add, "May I plant the seeds myself? I have taken good care of them this far."

"No. I will do it."

"But, Father, why not?"

"You have already done too much."

"Soaking seeds? I've done nothing! How I wish you would let me into the apothecary garden! I could help you with your research, your cures—"

"No! You must not. Swear to me, Jessamine. Even

29

when I am not home—and I may have to go away again, and soon—swear that you will not go in there." Father walks toward me step by step, forcing me to retreat until I stand in the doorway to the study once more.

"You needn't make me swear. The gate is locked, remember?" I sound sullen and sarcastic; I cannot help it. "For I am only a foolish child who cannot be trusted to have sense enough not to poison herself. Isn't that what you think? But you are mistaken, Father. I am not a child anymore."

"You are a child," Father says flatly, "until I say you are not. Now leave me. I will see you at supper."

He steps back, and the ancient door shuts in my face.

Out the front door of the cottage, through the court-yard, past the ruins and the outer wall, to the footpath, the crossroads, the world. I walk quickly, until my breath comes fast and my heart pounds.

I may not go back. No—I *will* not go back. If Father

can disappear for three days, so can I. For three days, or three years, or three lifetimes.

You are a child until I say you are not.

Am I really? What child would leave home as I do now, with no destination except away from you, penniless and provisionless, with only the shawl around her head for shelter?

When I grow hungry I will find roots and berries to eat. Perhaps it is out here, in the wide, wild, unchained world, that I will finally taste all the forbidden fruit you keep under lock and key. Perhaps there are fresh mysteries growing in the woods, delicious, dangerous poisons that even you do not know exist!

In this way my spiteful, wounded thoughts circle round and round, erasing the passage of time. Am I a mile from the cottage? Five miles? Ten? I break into a half run as the path veers into a downhill slope, and spread my arms like a sail to catch the wind. If only the currents of air could lift me and carry me! How pleasant it would be to fly on that wind, like the tuft of a dandelion. How much easier it would be to soar, weightless, than to trudge across the countryside dragging the bulk of my long skirt and petticoat, with my feet bound into heavy boots that seem to have grown too small, again.

I pause to catch my breath and to still my whirling brain. My thoughts trip over one another, vying to be heard, like many voices in a shouting mob. My hair has come loose and the stinging tendrils whip into my eyes. The hem of my skirt is heavy with mud; my sleeves are damp with the tears I have been wiping away since I bolted from the cottage. I did not think to bring water with me—I was not thinking at all when I ran out in the heat of fury—and now my throat is raw and dry.

It would serve Father right if I sated my thirst from the ditch where I poured the belladonna water, I think bitterly. *Let him find me dead under the gorse bushes. Let him bury me deep in the ground, my arms twined around the bones of that soft, orange-furred cat.*

Exhausted, I let myself fall to the ground in the sheep meadow that borders the path. I lie with my back pressed to the earth and feel the dampness of the grass seeping into my clothes.

Above me, high in the cold blue sky, a black dot moves, first one way, then another, making wide, deliberate zigzags toward the earth. As it descends, it grows larger, grows wings, grows a voice.

It is a raven, and its raspy cry mocks my own dry sobs. It lands on a fence post by the path, ten paces up the slope from me. Proudly it flexes its great black wings; when fully open, they span nearly as far as I can spread my own two arms. Its sleek head gleams with an iridescent, oily sheen.

I lift myself up on my elbows. In answer, the bird cocks its head to the side so I can admire its lifeless black eye, set like a black pearl in the side of its skull. It repeats its raw cry—a terrible, merciless cry.

Kraaaaaaaaaaaaaaaaaaaah!

The sheep bleat in fear and move away. The raven hunkers down into itself and gathers its energy to spring. It has decided on a target, chosen a victim—a young lamb that has wandered too far from the flock—

In a flash I am on my feet, a stone in my hand. With all my might I hurl it at the raven. My aim is low, and the stone hits the post with a sharp *thwack*. The bird flaps its wings clumsily in surprise and rises on taut, wiry legs. It swivels its head to look at me full on.

I hurl another stone. This time I hit the bird squarely, right on its oily black chest.

KRAAAAAAAAAAAAAH!

The raven screams in fury and takes flight, circling around and swooping low over my head. I fall to the ground and curl in a ball, covering my face with the shawl.

Go ahead, wicked bird, I think, *try to peck out my eyes if you can. Even blinded, I will grab you by the throat and never let go. I am that angry and reckless now, and I care nothing for what happens to me.*

As if hearing my thoughts, the raven retreats, still complaining, until its furious cry fades into the sky.

I uncurl my body and look around. The sheep stare at me, their limpid, nearly human eyes wet with gratitude.

I shiver with cold and fatigue, and my knees weaken with the relief that comes when danger has passed.

It has passed for the lamb, perhaps. For now. But not for me.

Finally I let myself feel all the fear and sorrow in my heart, and my tears are set loose once more. *I am easy prey,* I think, *a motherless lamb, alone in the world. No flock, no friends, no green field I can call home. And the skies are full of ravens.*

I have no choice. I must go back to Hulne Abbey.

During my wild race from home, rage and hurt blotted out all sense of time passed or distance traveled—but now, on the shame-filled journey back, the movement of the clock resumes with vengeful slowness. It is a full three hours before I reach the cottage. For the final torturous hour I must pick my footing step by step in the pitch dark, for of course I have no lantern. Twice I stumble and catch myself on my hands, leaving my palms scraped bloody from the gravelly path.

Easy prey, my fear whispers to me with every step. *Remember what you are.*

The cottage is cold and dark when I finally cross its threshold, with only a few glowing remnants of a fire glowing among the ashes in the parlor hearth. If there has been a supper I have missed it, but with no one to cook or call him to the table, Father may well still be working, reading and muttering, oblivious to all that has taken place outside the locked world of his study.

I light a candle and rummage in the pantry until I find a leftover boiled egg and some cold cooked potato. I wrap them in a linen napkin to take upstairs with me. I will eat them in private and then go to sleep, to put the memory of this awful day behind me as quickly as I can.

The house is so quiet; perhaps Father has already retired to bed. Out of habit I pause to check the pail by the back door, the one marked POISON that holds the belladonna seeds. Tonight is their last night soaking in this watery womb. Tomorrow they will be planted, in the garden where I am not permitted to go.

I lift the lid and lower my candle so I can see inside.

The bucket is dry and empty. The belladonna seeds are gone.

My first, horrified thought: *Has someone stolen them? Father will be furious!*

But then I listen again: The cottage is silent, but there are noises coming from outside. Dull, digging noises. The sound of earth being turned.

Now that I no longer need its light, the moon has risen and bathed the courtyard in its soft glow. But I do not have to see my way. I know exactly where to go. Past the courtyard, past the fishpond, past all the garden beds, up the narrow winding path to the left that leads to the tall, locked gate.

I lay one hand on the rough metal chain; with the other I clasp the lock. I press my forehead against the cold iron bars, and peer through the dark forms and moving shadows of a mysterious world I will never be allowed to enter.

Father is at the north wall, bent over in the moonlight, digging. Whistling softly. Happy.

Silently I return to the cottage. I stand by the back door, my head hanging down in defeat.

Without my bidding, my foot lashes out and kicks over the empty pail.

Will everything I care for be taken away from me?

4

23rd March

A fine, clear day, but a sharp metal smell in the air
warns of a coming storm.

I planted more radishes in the morning, also set
bulbs of onions and garlic. The bulbs overwintered
nicely in the cellar; they were dry and firm, with no
sign of mold.

Took out my mending basket to repair torn
stockings and found a

THE SOUND OF HOOFBEATS seems to come from nowhere, and gets louder so quickly I drop my pen to the floor in surprise. Father did not say that we would be receiving company, and now I cannot recall if the beds are made—

The hoofbeats get closer by the second. They must be headed here, for the nearest farm is two miles in the other direction.

"Father!" I call, as I half run to the kitchen to put away the breakfast things. "Someone is coming! Shall I prepare a meal? Shall I make tea?"

It has been almost a week since Father stole (for in my mind he did steal them) and planted the belladonna seeds. We have not spoken of it, nor have we spoken of much else in the intervening days. But the excitement of an unexpected guest makes me forget my resolve to punish him with my silence.

"Father!" I call more loudly. "Are you expecting company?"

We do not get many visitors at the cottage, only the occasional tradesman trying to sell us tin pots or a matron from a neighboring farm seeking a cure for the toothache. But every now and again the duke himself will appear, unannounced, with a small hunting party in tow. This land is the duke's land, as is most of the acreage in Northumberland, and the fields and forests that spread over the site of the old monastery have long been the duke's favorite hunting park. After an afternoon's shooting, he and his guests have sometimes stopped here to gaze at the ruins, water their horses, and brag about the day's kill.

Father lurches into the parlor with his hair standing every which way, as if he had spent hours running his hands through it in deep concentration. "I expect no one. And I do not wish to be disturbed, so whoever it is, bid them be gone."

"But what if it is the duke?"

He listens. The hoofbeats are insistent, a hard gallop coming straight this way.

His face turns grim. "Whoever comes travels alone, and at reckless speed. It is not the duke, but it might be a highwayman. Stand back from the door, Jessamine."

Father grabs his gun from the wooden box on the floor beside the entrance to the cottage, and unbolts the heavy arched wooden door.

He steps out into the courtyard. I am frightened, but my curiosity is greater than my fear, and I follow. We emerge just in time to see our visitor gallop up and pull his horse to an abrupt stop directly in front of our door, raising a choking cloud of dust.

The horse has been ridden too hard for too long; its mouth drips foam, and its neck and flanks are flecked with sweat. It whinnies and rears high in complaint at the brutal pull on the reins. The rider curses and yanks the horse's head hard around.

I sneak closer behind Father so I can get a glimpse of our uninvited guest. He is a long-limbed, pock-faced man. Lashed to the saddle behind him is a large, shapeless bundle wrapped in a threadbare blanket and tied around with rope.

The man slips off the horse's back and lands heavily on the ground. "Thomas Luxton?" he barks. "The apothecary?"

"I am he." Behind his back, Father's hand tightens on the gun.

"May I speak to you, sir?"

"You already have, *sir*." Father seems to double in size until he fills the doorway. "What is your business? You arrive like a fire wagon racing to put out a blaze. But as you can see"—Father gestures in such a way as to reveal his weapon—"we have no need of assistance."

At the sight of the gun, the man steps back. Then he sees me hiding behind Father. For a split second our eyes meet. I know mine are filled with fear.

He sighs and stamps the mud off his boots, then reaches up to remove his three-cornered hat. He wears a wig, as is the fashion, but when he takes off the hat he knocks his wig slightly askew. Suddenly I am no longer afraid, for how can one be afraid of a man in a crooked wig?

"Forgive me," he says gruffly. "There is no need to defend yourself; I mean you no harm. My name is Tobias Pratt. I am sorry to disturb you and will not stay one moment longer than necessary. But I ask that you let me enter your home briefly, so that you and I may speak—in private."

When he says "in private," I think he must mean out of my hearing, for who else is here but Father and me? But the bundle on the back of Pratt's horse stirs.

"Water," it moans. Whether the voice is young or old, male or female, I cannot say.

"Shut your mouth, boy. You've had plenty of water today." Pratt turns back to Father. "What I have to say will be of interest to you, Luxton, I swear it. Will you hear me out?"

Father says nothing but stares at the pitiful, rag-swaddled creature on the horse.

"Water," it moans again, but this time quite low and sad, as if it has no hope of being heard.

I would fetch the creature some water; what harm could there be in that? I am about to ask permission to do so when Father speaks.

"As you wish," he says abruptly. "Come inside and say what you have to say. The sooner you are gone, the

44

sooner I can get back to my work."

"Father, ought I to get some water for . . . ?" I nod my head in the direction of the horse and its strange burden.

"Leave the monster be for now," Pratt interjects. "After you hear my tale, you may do with it what you will."

"Tobias Pratt—your name is familiar to me; why is that?" Father and our visitor are seated at the table. I have already made the tea. Quickly and silently I put some biscuits on a dish, and stand aside to listen.

"I am the founder and proprietor of Pratt's Convalescent Home," Pratt says proudly as he shoves two biscuits at once into his mouth. "I imagine you've heard of it. It is a respected establishment here in the north."

"Indeed I have." Father waves away my offer of tea, so I pour a cup for Pratt and take my seat in the shadows. "You run a madhouse in the countryside, a few miles west of Haydon Bridge, do you not?"

Pratt shrugs. "Call it a madhouse if you will. I prefer to think of it as a safe and comfortable refuge for the mentally unhinged. Pratt's Home has always been a well-run institution and, if I may say, a profitable business, too. We take all comers, as long as their families can pay: lunatics, melancholics, would-be poets who've addled their brains with laudanum. We see quite a lot of that type lately, in fact."

Pratt forces a smile that looks more like a grimace. One of his two front teeth is missing; the other is rotten and black, and the stink of his breath reaches even to where I sit, on my small stool near the fire. He pushes back his chair and stretches out his spindly legs. "So you see, you and I are both medical men, after a fashion, Luxton."

The disgust on Father's face is impossible to miss. "I consider myself a plantsman, first and foremost. And you sound more like a banker than a healer, frankly. But now I know who you are, and how you earn your keep. So I ask you again: What brings you to my door, Mr. Pratt?"

"I have a story to tell you." Pratt drains his tea and puts the cup down with so much force it rattles the dishes. "And a gift for you as well—although you may not want it, after you hear what I have to say."

A thin blue vein throbs in a crooked line down the center of Father's forehead. "A gift I may not want?" he says coldly. "You are trying to intrigue me, Pratt. That alone is enough to make me show you the door, for I dislike being played with. If you have something to say, say it, and make sure it's the plain truth while you're at it. I have no patience for elaboration."

For a moment Pratt looks as if he would try to argue; to his credit he thinks better of it. "Have it your way, Luxton. The plain truth it shall be. My tale is about a boy. A foundling boy, an orphan, no doubt. He's a strange, half-grown lad. I don't know how old; at a glance I'd say about as old as your daughter here— this is your daughter, is it not?" He jerks a thumb in my direction. "She's a bit young to be a wife, to my way of thinking, but to each his own."

I feel my cheeks redden. "The girl is no part of

your tale; leave her out of it, if you please," Father says harshly.

Pratt lifts his hands in apology and continues. "I meant no offense. This boy I speak of—he came to live with me nearly two months ago. Before that he'd been raised by a local friar; before the friar, God only knows where he was whelped. He's not much to look at, a skittish, wild-eyed sort of waif. You know the type: flinches when you speak to him, never lifts his eyes from his shoes, a body so thin a strong wind could snap him in two like a dead branch."

"The company of poets has taken its toll on you, Pratt," Father says wryly. "Judging from your description, this urchin hardly seems a worthwhile addition to your household. Why did you take him in to begin with?"

Pratt squirms. "Well, you know how it is. There's no end to the work in my business, and an extra set of hands is always welcome. And the scrawny ragamuffin scarcely ate, so he was no expense to keep. He never took any gruel or bread. Now and then I'd catch him eating a bit of rabbit or pigeon he'd caught on his own. I let him sleep in the coal bin and put him to work gathering firewood and doing errands for the cook."

"So you took the child as an unpaid servant," Father observes. "A slave, to put it bluntly."

"Better that than freezing by the roadside!" Pratt retorts. "I could tell right off he was an odd one, but he did his work without complaint. After he got his bearings, one day he asks if he might start bringing in the afternoon tea for the patients. Like a fool I let him."

"A fool?" Father interjects sharply. "In what way?"

Pratt wrings his hands as if he is trying to wring the words out of himself. "A fool, yes . . . I wonder what you will make of this, Luxton—the wretched brat cured my inmates!"

"*Cured* them—of what?"

"Of their madness! What else is there to cure a madman of?" Pratt rises from his chair and paces around the small room. "Mind you, these were hard cases. Babbling, gibbering maniacs who'd wrap their hands around your throat if you looked at them sideways. Women who cackled like hyenas and tore their hair from the roots. But within a fortnight after the boy arrived, the worst of the lot were lolling about the garden, reading the *Times* and exchanging pleasantries!" He leans close to Father. "Here's the meat of it, Luxton: I'm convinced the brat put something in the tea."

Silence, except for the crackle and sputter of the fire.

"Fascinating," Father finally says, in a level voice. "What do you suppose it was?"

"Who knows? Who cares? Straightaway I told the witch boy, 'Whatever tonic you're brewing in that kettle of yours, I order you to put an end to it now. If England runs out of madmen I'll soon go out of business, and that means you'll be out of a home once more; how would you like that, you wretched pup?' Well, I thought I'd made my point clear as day, and that'd be the end of it—but the lad said nothing, just stared at his feet nodding."

"And then?"

"That was two weeks ago. My inmates—those that are left—are docile as doves, but half the town has gone mad." Pratt wipes the sweat from his forehead with his soiled sleeve. "Respectable matrons running unclothed in the streets. Grown men jumping off rooftops, screaming, 'I can fly, I can fly!' Now people are starting to look upon my business with suspicion. As if madness were contagious!"

It might only be the play of firelight on his features, but to me it looks almost as if Father is trying not to laugh. "Shocking," he remarks, not sounding particularly surprised. "And did the boy have anything to say about this development?"

"I asked him, you may be sure," Pratt says, clenching his fists. "I had to find him first; the guilty wretch had disappeared. I searched high and low, until I found him lying in a hayfield, happy as you please. I lifted him up by the shirtfront and shook him hard, and demanded to know what devilment he'd wrought this time! And hear what he says, in his smug, simpering voice: 'I know nothing of devils,

Master, but I did speak to an angel once.' The cheek! So I shouted at him, right in his face so there'd be no mistaking my mood, 'Don't talk to me of angels! The whole town has gone loony!' And the imp shrugs his bony shoulders and says, 'Business will be picking up then.' You see what I've been up against."

Exhausted, Pratt collapses into his seat at the table again, and props his head in his hands.

The light from the fire leaps and flickers. I burn too, with curiosity; what does Father make of this outlandish tale? He says nothing for a long time, and then gestures to me.

"I believe I am ready for that tea now, Jessamine."

I leap up and pour. Father stirs his cup idly for a moment and then raises his eyes to Pratt.

"Who is this boy? Where does he come from?"

Pratt shakes his head. "No family that anyone knows of, or that he'll admit to. As I said, he was living with a local friar when I came into possession of him. He answers to the name of Weed. It suits him, if you ask me."

"And where is the friar now?"

Pratt glances at me, then looks away. "Dead. The friar died in his sleep, with no sign of illness as warning and only this boy as witness."

Father stands. I can see from his face that he has had enough of this man. "It is an outlandish story, to be sure," he says. "But I am confused; you mentioned something about a gift?"

"I mean the boy, Luxton. That's him tied up on the back of my horse. I want you to take him off my hands."

I bite my lip so as not to let out a yelp of surprise, but I bite too hard and the taste of blood fills my mouth. *But Pratt called him "monster," I think. Surely Papa will say no?*

Father crosses to the fire. He does not warm his hands but stands gazing into the leaping yellow flames. Without turning his head, he answers, "After all that you have just told me, what reason could I possibly have to give this Weed of yours a home?"

Pratt glances at me again, then turns back to

Father and speaks in a low voice. "I know a bit about you, Luxton. People in my line of work, we talk to one another. I've heard about what your interests are, the research you do, your potions, your 'experiments'—"

"Enough!" Father snaps. "I will not listen to this gibberish. Go, and take your miserable stray with you."

Pratt rises and slaps his hat on his head. "The boy seems to know a thing or two about brewing a pot of tea. From what people say about you, I thought that might be reason enough to pique your interest." He turns as he reaches the door. "Tell you what: You take him in and find out for yourself if he's any worth to you. Then we'll talk price. Once you've satisfied your curiosity, I don't care what you do with him. Nor will anyone else; he's a weed to be sure. Dispose of him as you wish."

"A strange gift, indeed," Father says, stroking his chin. "Very well. Only time will tell whether thanks— or payment—are in order, so you will excuse me for not offering either just yet."

"You'll take him, then?" Pratt seems both relieved and incredulous.

"For a while, at least."

"You're not afraid?"

Father smiles. "From what you say, Pratt, he's only a youth, and a dimwitted one at that. The deeds you accuse him of would require knowledge that few people possess, not to mention a deceitful and murderous spirit. The poor wretch hardly sounds capable."

Pratt shakes his head. "For your sake, Luxton, I hope you're right. But if you want my advice—keep him out of the kitchen."

With that, Pratt strides to the door. Father and I follow him outside. The huddled figure still teeters and sways on the back of Pratt's horse. Without offering so much as a word, Pratt unties the bundle from the saddle, lifts it off the horse, and heaves it to the ground.

As he does I catch a glimpse—a tangled mess of black hair above a pale, high forehead.

Pratt untethers his horse and swings himself up

and astride. He looks down at Father and me, and then at the piteous figure in the dirt. For a moment it seems as if he might say some words of farewell.

"Hey-ah!" he grunts, then kicks his horse hard, and they are off.

Father and I stand wordlessly as the hoofbeats fade into the distance. A passing cloud covers the sun and sends a sudden chill across the courtyard.

"It is a shame your former master left in such a hurry," Father remarks to the mysterious figure on the ground. "It seems he was eager to be rid of you. Yet with a few minutes of friendly conversation we might have persuaded you to tell him exactly what it was that you dumped in the village well."

There is movement, wriggling. The mummylike wrapping loosens. First the dark, tousled hair emerges, followed by the high, pale forehead. Then two wide emerald green eyes appear.

My breath catches in my chest at the sight. I have never seen such beautiful eyes—like twin jewels. No monster could possess features of such beauty. All my fear of this new arrival dissolves in an instant.

Those hypnotic green eyes stare at Father, expressionless as glass.

"Was it monkshood, perhaps? Or angel's trumpet? No matter; someone will figure it out eventually, though a few delirious villagers may leap to their deaths in the meantime. And you are called Weed, eh?" Father opens the door of the cottage and gestures for Weed to enter. "The perfect name for an unwanted sprout like you. Now unswaddle yourself from those rags, and come inside. I wish to discover exactly what sort of a gift you are."

5

25th March

The weather has shifted. The breeze is warm and full of promise.

No time to write more. I have to tend to Weed.

TODAY IS THE FIRST DAY of a new season.

It is the season of Weed.

He is not much company yet. All day and all night he hides in the coal bin, hunched and silent. Father says it must be because that is what he was accustomed to at the madhouse, but I think Father may have frightened him with his wild talk of throwing poison into wells; it is no wonder he does not wish to speak to us. So far he has refused to eat most of the food I bring, though he will drink as much water as he is offered.

I will be patient. Any wild creature can be tamed, if you are willing to wait and be still. I have learned this from the feral cats that lurk around the courtyard. They stare like yellow-eyed demons; they bolt and hide if you approach, but sooner or later, when they are hungry enough, they come and take the food from your hand.

So it will be with Weed—but not yet. In the meantime I have decided that I will introduce myself to him, to get him accustomed to my presence. He may not answer me at first, but that is no matter. I have someone to talk to, at last! My words will be like sunshine and air. My voice will rain down on him, and then we shall see what glorious orchid may blossom from this shy, unwanted Weed.

I race through my chores in half the usual time so that I may spend the rest of the day taming my new friend. Since he will not leave the coal bin, I carry my small stool down to the cellar and sit as close as I dare.

"My name is Jessamine Luxton," I say, as a way to begin. "I am sixteen years of age. My father is Thomas Luxton, the apothecary. You met him already; he was the one that picked you up off the ground and brought you inside the cottage, after that dreadful man on horseback left you lying in the dirt like rubbish."

While I speak he stays facing away from me, his body curved around his knees as if he were encased in the hard husk of a seed.

"So," I say, nudging my stool an inch closer, "now you have met Father and me. That means you have met my whole family, for my mother is dead, and I am an only child. My father and I live here alone together."

I see a finger twitch, flex.

"This place we live in, this house, which I call our cottage—it is very old. Some would say it is a sacred place. The Catholic monks used to live and worship here."

He turns, and his mouth moves as if he would speak.

"*Bells*," he breathes.

His voice is so soft it is not even a whisper. More like the rustle of a leaf.

"Yes," I say encouragingly, in case I heard right. "Centuries ago, in this very place, there were church bells ringing, and Mass bells, and the call to vespers. When the monastery was here there must have been bells ringing all the time."

"*Bells*."

I am nearly sure that is what he said, but it was so soft, a mere flutter of air. "Bells?" I repeat gently. "Do you mean Canterbury bells? They are such pretty flowers, I grow them in my cutting garden."

Weed's whole face brightens. "Garden?" he asks, quite clearly.

His green eyes pierce me like emerald daggers. "Do you like gardens? We have many," I say in a rush.

"In the kitchen gardens I grow all our vegetables and herbs for the table, and there is a small orchard for fruit, and a bee garden so the bees will make delicious honey, and a dye garden so I can make dyes to color the wool. And Father has his apothecary garden of plants that he uses to make medicines and cures—but we may not enter there, for Father's work is secret, and many of those plants are poison—"

"Jessamine!" Father stands silhouetted at the top of the cellar stairs. "What on earth are you telling that boy?"

"Nothing—"

"Do not lie, Jessamine. I heard you speaking. A person cannot speak nothing."

"I am sorry, Father. I should have said, 'Nothing of importance,'" I reply with false cheer, to cover the shame I feel at being scolded in front of Weed. "I was telling Weed about us, and our home, and about the gardens—he ought to know where he is, and in whose care, oughtn't he?"

Father ignores my reply. "Since he is ready to

speak, bring the boy upstairs to my study. At once, please." Then he leaves, letting the door close behind him. The shaft of daylight coming down the stairwell is snuffed out.

I take a deep breath to compose myself and give my eyes time to adjust to the sudden darkness. Then I make myself smile reassuringly at Weed. "Father can be stern, but you mustn't be frightened of him. Will you come upstairs?"

I extend my hand. Weed takes it and rises gracefully to his feet, unfolding his long legs in a single fluid motion. The dim light gives his pale face an unearthly beauty that takes my breath away—the dark, unkempt hair, his wide, impossibly green eyes, his weightless form as willowy as a sapling.

"Come," I say, steadying my voice. "Perhaps he will let you see the belladonna berries; they are quite lovely. He keeps some in a jar on the shelf."

"Belladonna," Weed says, looking at me so intensely his green eyes nearly light up the dark. "A beautiful lady."

I know he does not mean me, but I blush anyway, and go first up the stairs so he cannot see my scarlet face.

Father sits behind his desk, scribbling in one of his notebooks, but when I bring Weed into the study he slams the book shut and springs to his feet.

"Sit down, boy," he says, not unkindly. He pulls an armchair next to the desk and gestures for Weed to take it. I perch in the window seat. "If you are to live under my roof, I must know some things about you. Will you do your best to answer my questions?"

Weed glances at me, then at Father, and gives a slight nod.

"You go by the name of Weed. Do you have any other name?"

Weed shakes his head no.

"Any family? Parents, brothers, sisters?"

No.

"And what about that Tobias Pratt? He was kind to you? He was like a father to you, perhaps? You must

64

have grown very attached to him."

Weed lifts his eyes and gazes steadily at Father.

"No," he says. "He is an awful man."

Father nods. "Excellent. Telling the truth will serve you well, with me, and elsewhere, too. Now I wish to ask you about the friar you once lived with. Do you know who I mean?"

"Yes," Weed's voice slowly gains confidence. "Friar Bartholomew."

"You did like him, I can see it on your face."

Weed nods. "He cared for me."

"How long did you live with him?"

"For as many seasons as I can remember." Weed glances at me before adding, "He found me in a basket."

Father nods. "It was once the custom to leave foundling children on the doorstep of the monasteries. Perhaps someone thought a friar would do just as well in a pinch. Now I must ask you, Weed: This Friar Bartholomew—was he a secret Catholic? You can tell me the truth; the man is already dead, so no further harm can come to him."

I realize what Father is thinking: If this friar posed as an Anglican but secretly practiced the old faith, he might have been a repository for the ancient wisdom of the monks. Perhaps the friar was a hidden link in a long, secret chain, preserving the knowledge that was thought to have been lost centuries ago—the knowledge Father has sought all his life.

Weed shrugs.

"Does that mean yes, or no?" Impatience creeps into Father's voice.

"I don't know," Weed says flatly. "I don't know if he had a secret."

Father walks back and forth, caged by his own frustration. "Did this Bartholomew have any books, Weed? Old, musty books, perhaps? Books having to do with plants?"

"No."

Father stops pacing and fixes Weed with a look. "This is important, Weed. This knowledge is priceless. If you knew of the existence of such books, it would not be right to keep it to yourself."

"No books."

"Are you sure?"

"Friar Bartholomew kept no books," Weed says firmly. "Just beer."

That silences Father, but not for long. He strides across the room and back again, pauses, and then pulls up a chair very close to where Weed sits. He slips into the chair and regards Weed with a friendly, open expression.

"Weed, Mr. Pratt says you know how to prepare certain types of medicines. He claims you made a special tea, one that has the power to calm a sick mind."

Weed shakes his head, *no no no no.*

"It is all right," Father says quickly. "It is not wrong to know how to do these things. Forget how Pratt scolded you; he is a brute and a fool, a condition for which I fear there will never be a cure." He gestures around his study. "I prepare many types of medicines myself, Weed. I would not punish you for doing the same. Now tell me," Father presses on.

"What did you put in that tea? How did you know which plants to use, and in what quantities? And if you did not gain this knowledge from books, or from your beer-soaked friar, then from where?"

"I made the tea, yes," Weed replies carefully.

"How, Weed? Who told you how to cure the inmates?"

I can hear how hard Father is trying to mask his impatience, but the vein on his forehead is beginning to throb. Inwardly I will him to be gentle.

Weed presses his lips together and says no more. Father leans closer. His voice grows more urgent. "Who taught you how to poison the well water?"

Weed leaps to his feet; he looks ready to bolt. "No! I did not poison anyone—"

"Father." I step forward and lay a hand on his arm. "I'm sure he will tell us everything in time. First we must earn his trust."

Father looks at Weed, then back at me. The blue vein in his forehead goes taut momentarily but quickly fades.

"You are perfectly correct, Jessamine." He stands. "For now our only purpose should be to make certain Weed is happy here. He must be well fed, well cared for, and safe. He needs time—time to become part of the family. After all," he adds, to Weed, "families have no need to keep secrets from one another, do they, Weed?"

Weed stares at his feet. "I would not know, sir."

It has been nearly a week since Weed came to live here.

I have spent hours with him every day, in speech and in silence—every hour I can spare from my work in the gardens and the cottage. He no longer turns away when he sees me, and (I hope I am not imagining it!) he even seems to like it when I come. He always answers me when I talk to him, though his answers sometimes sound more like riddles.

Still, I am so used to being alone that even his moss green stare feels like eloquence to me. I tell him all the things I know, about the old monastery and hospital, the lost books of the monks, my work in the gardens, and Father's work as an apothecary. In truth I am afraid to stop talking, for if I do he may hear how my heart pounds and my breath quickens whenever I am near his strange, dark beauty. So I talk and talk, while Weed listens and gazes at me, unblinking as a cat. These conversations seem to satisfy us both.

But he will not go outside and has not ventured upstairs since his visit to Father's study. He takes water but will not touch most of the food I offer him. A hard-boiled egg, some broth, a slice of cured ham—this is all I have been able to persuade him to eat. Yesterday when I asked him why, all he said was, "I do not wish to hurt."

"What hurts?" I asked, alarmed. "Your stomach? Or a tooth, perhaps?" He shook his head and would say no more.

Today for breakfast I bring him a bowl of porridge, which he refuses. I ask him again: Why will he not eat? To my surprise he answers me.

"It is alive. It would hurt. It would be wrong."

70

"Alive? The porridge, you mean?"

He nods, and looks at the bowl with revulsion. "Oats."

I try not to smile. "When they were growing in the field, the oats were alive, I suppose. But they were harvested long ago. Now they are dried and cooked."

He shakes his head. "There is no difference."

This is a riddle, indeed. But I will solve it.

"What else is alive, then?" I ask. "Bread?"

"Yes."

"Turnips?"

"Yes."

"Carrots?"

"Yes."

"Raspberries? Apples?"

He nods.

"Bacon?"

He stops, thinks for a moment. "No."

I jump up. "Stay here; I will be back very soon."

I run to the storehouse and find some bacon. It takes me only a few minutes to fry it in the pan. The smell of it fills the house and drifts down to the cellar. By the time I return to Weed with a plate, his eyes are bright with expectation. He devours the thick, greasy slabs as I watch, trying to make sense of it all.

"Weed," I say gently when he is almost finished. "Why do you feel so strongly about the carrots and apples but not about the bacon?"

"Bacon," he says through a full mouth, "is not my friend."

I am overjoyed to see him eat, but Weed cannot live on bacon and hard-boiled eggs. For one thing, meat is costly and we do not have that much bacon put aside, and the chickens can only lay so many eggs each day.

But as I sit in the parlor, watching the sunlight filter through the many panes of those tall, arched chapel windows, an idea comes to me. I go into the root cellar and choose some fine, firm potatoes. Back in the kitchen, I peel and quarter them and drop them in a pot of boiling water. When they are cooked, I drain them and sprinkle them with coarse salt.

I put the boiled potatoes in a covered tureen, to keep them warm. I grab a small tin plate and fork and take the whole picnic downstairs to the coal bin.

"Weed, I cooked something for you."

"What is it?" he asks warily.

"Potatoes."

He turns away, disgusted. "No," he insists, shielding his mouth with his hands. "I cannot eat that."

"Yes you can. You must. There is a way to eat that is proper. Once you learn what it is, you will be able to enjoy all the fruits of the earth with no fear of harming any living thing: potatoes and carrots and apples, too."

Is that a flicker of hope in his eyes? The potatoes do smell delicious.

"What way is that?" he asks at last.

"With gratitude. You must learn to say grace. Like this." I demonstrate. "Thank you for all that I am about to receive." Slowly I place the potato in my mouth.

He looks away, repulsed. I remain calm.

"See?" I say after I swallow. "Nothing bad happens. Now you must try."

With trembling fingers, he takes a piece of boiled potato. The first time I say the words with him: "Thank you for all that I am about to receive."

He takes a small bite and then stops, as if he does not know what to do next.

"Again," I gently urge. "Say it."

"Thank you for all that I am about to receive." Weed takes another bite, chews, swallows.

"See? It is all right." I let him hold the tureen. "It is what nature intends."

"Thank you for all that I am about to receive." A new expression crosses his face as he eats. I can see it in his eyes, the flood of ecstatic feeling as the food hits his empty belly.

"Thank you for all that I am about—"

"You don't need to say it before every bite," I interrupt. "Just once before dinner is fine."

He nods, and shoves more potato in his mouth.

74

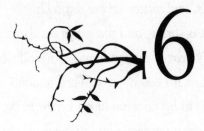

6

8th April

A fine, clear day. The sun shines with a welcoming
light.

Everywhere the trees shyly display their newly
opened leaves, so tender and green. The willow
tree is already in bloom, heavy with catkins. The
rhododendron buds have swollen to bursting; razor
edges of pink and violet show through at each seam.
New blossoms appear in the meadow every day
and make a kaleidoscope of the grass: bluebells,

violets, and butter-yellow daffodils.

It is spring, and the world awakens. I can hardly bear to stay indoors—I would sleep beneath the stars if I could—but Weed remains dormant, buried in his coal bin like a kernel in the husk.

I must persuade him to awaken, too.

"HOW OLD ARE YOU, WEED?" I ask when I bring down his breakfast: a bowl of porridge, a boiled egg, two apples and two strips of bacon, tea, and a cup of fresh milk. Now that he has made his peace with eating grains and fruit, he eats a great deal. I thought he was younger than I am when I first saw him bundled up in those rags, but now, as he gains color and flesh, I suspect he may be my age, at least.

He tucks the napkin under his chin and shrugs. "How old is the grass?"

His breakfast tray rests on a plank of wood we prop across the coal bin; he sits on the stool, and I perch on the bottommost stair. "Your question has no answer," I say in return. "The grass dies every winter and comes back every spring. It has no age in years; it is both newborn and everlasting."

"That must be how old I am, then." He lifts his fork and recites, "Thank you for all I am about to receive."

"So you are as old as grass, and as young as grass?" I tease. He does not smile.

"The truth is I do not know," he says after a moment. "Found in a basket by a drunken friar is not much of a birthday."

"From now on, then, the loveliest day of spring can be your birthday," I say impulsively. "And you can be my age. Sixteen now, seventeen next month. That means you are older than I am, for I do not turn seventeen until autumn."

"Sixteen," he repeats. "All right."

He eats, and I watch. After a few minutes he offers me a slice of apple.

"Thank you." I take it between two fingers and lift it to my lips.

"Eh!" he cries. "First you must say it—"

"Thank you for all I am about to receive," I say

obligingly, and pop the apple slice in my mouth.

It takes him only a short while to finish every bite on the tray. "Come." I hold out my hand. "The sky is the most wonderful shade of blue. You must come upstairs with me, and we will take a walk in the meadow."

He drops his fork. "I like it down here," he replies.

"But you must come see! The tulips are in bloom, and there are rowan trees growing from the ruins."

"I like the quiet," he says softly.

"It is quiet outdoors, too. All one hears are the pleasant sounds of the world going about its business: the wind blowing, and the sheep bleating, and the meadow grass rustling in the wind." I lean forward so my face is close to his, and whisper, "If you prefer it to be quiet, I will not say a word, I promise."

He pays no attention to me. Instead he gazes up at the cellar door, which I had left ajar when I came downstairs, as I needed both hands to hold the breakfast tray. A barely perceptible current of air wafts down to us.

Weed closes his eyes and breathes in the clean scent of spring. Then he cocks his head, as if listening.

"All right," he agrees. "It is time."

Father's old shirt is loose on Weed but otherwise suits him well. The trousers are too long, so I help him roll them up at the leg. There is no need for a coat today; the sun soaks into our skin until it feels as if the warmth radiates from our very bones.

We walk slowly. In my mind, I explain every detail of my world to him: how the fishpond, now drained and covered with a heavy wooden board, once served as a place to store live fish until they were to be eaten. How, as summer comes, the clematis vines will climb and weave all over the ruined walls inside the courtyard and turn them into flowering monuments, blanketed in deep purple and crimson.

I could point out the marigolds that must be moved into a sunnier spot this year, and the patch of bee balm that has grown too big and needs to be divided. Too, I could show him the path up the slope that leads to

Father's locked apothecary garden, where we may not enter, though I suppose we could go look through the gate if Weed is curious.

But I promised to be quiet, so I do not speak of these things. Would he even care about them? I do not know; whatever opinions he has are hidden away behind the locked gates of his own silent lips.

Once we cross the courtyard and pass through the outer wall, the view of the countryside opens up before us. There are sheep meadows on either side, cresting over the softly rolling hills like waves. In the distance lies the deep green mystery of the forest.

As we proceed along the path, Weed's eyes rove over the landscape as if they would devour it. We pass a copse of trees, so intimately arranged they seem to be leaning in to whisper secrets to one another.

Even as I think it, Weed pauses, then smiles.

"Look at the trees," he says.

"Like silly old gossips," I reply. He looks at me quizzically, and we continue in silence until our tranquil walk is disturbed by a ruckus in the hedgerow up ahead.

A stoat has seized a rabbit by the back of the neck. The rabbit, fat and helpless, emits a desperate squeal as they roll together, the rabbit trying to shake off the stoat, the stoat hanging fiercely onto the rabbit's back.

The stoat's long, flexible body reminds me of a snake, the way it curves and twists to hold tightly to its prey as they thrash in the dirt. The rabbit is nearly twice the size of its attacker, but the stoat has locked its teeth with vicious purpose. It hangs on by the scruff, just as a mother cat would do to carry her kittens to safety.

But the stoat intends something else. It will not let go until the rabbit's spine has snapped and its terrified eyes go glassy with death.

Easy prey. The words come to mind unbidden.

"The stoat should say grace," Weed observes, and walks on.

The tone of his voice makes me shiver—yet, of course, the stoat must eat. I remember Father's words: *That is the way of things. . . . Nature always gets her prize in the end.*

Keeping my eyes fixed ahead of me, I follow Weed and do not look back. After ten paces, I can barely hear the dying squeals of the rabbit. Twenty paces more and I cannot hear any of it—*the tearing of sinew, the snap of bone, the ecstatic wet sounds of the stoat gorging itself*—

Now all is still. There is only the rustling of the grass, the bleating of the sheep, and the soft, even tread of Weed's feet upon the path.

Weed strides along until we reach a large circle of stones. He stops and looks around with a puzzled expression.

"What is this place?" he demands.

I know the answer, but I am reluctant to speak of such unpleasant things during Weed's first exploration of Hulne Park. I take a breath and reply: "There was a hospital here once, many centuries ago. It was run by the monks, who knew a great deal about healing the sick. This stone circle is what is left of the place where the hospital disposed of its waste." I pause. "The drains from the operating rooms emptied here."

"Drains? For blood, you mean?"

"Yes, for the blood of the patients who were oper-
ated on." I look down at the grassy depression before
us. "This is where they buried the leeches that had
sucked on diseased flesh, and the limbs that were
removed because of infection or injury."

To my relief, Weed seems unperturbed.

"Sometimes Father likes to look about and see if
anything unusual grows from the earth," I add.

"I see," Weed says. "It is quiet here."

I find it no quieter than any other pile of rocks in
a field, but if the particular silence of this place pleases
Weed, then I am pleased as well.

"We can go back now," he says, turning around. "I
have walked enough for one day."

I do not want our excursion to end, not yet. When we
nearly reach the cottage I point straight ahead. "There
is another garden that way. We cannot go in it, but I
can show you where it is."

"All right," he says with a touch of wariness.

I lead him down the path that curves off to the left of the cottage, sloping briefly downhill and then climbing up the northernmost slope of the old monastery lands.

I look over my shoulder. Weed is lagging behind.

"Shall we turn back?"

There is a strange, haunted expression on his face. "We are almost there," he murmurs. It is not a question.

"Yes," I agree. "This is the apothecary garden. It is Father's special garden."

I gesture ahead as we come around the crest of the path. There is the tall black gate, the heavy chain, the iron lock. Behind the gate, the forbidden plants sway in the breeze, as if beckoning us inside—*slip through the gate, you can do it—come inside now—*

Weed looks stricken. He clasps both hands to his head, covering his ears.

"What is wrong?" I cry. "What do you hear?"

He shakes his head and lets out a sharp cry of pain.

84

I am afraid; what on earth is happening to him?

"Enough; we will go home," I say, pulling him away from the gate. "You must be exhausted; it is too much for your first day out. Can you make it to the cottage?"

He nods and lets me wrap a supportive arm around his back as he rests his arm upon my shoulder. In this way we make slow progress. With each step we take away from the gate he regains strength.

I am distraught to see him suffer, but there is something thrilling about the way he leans upon me as we make our way home. Even after we enter the cottage and he is nearly himself again, the weight and warmth of Weed's touch seems to linger on my skin.

I bring Weed some fresh water to drink, which revives him fully. Then I quickly prepare the evening meal.

When the food is ready, I call Father from his study. I am excited, for this will be the first time the three of us will share a dinner together.

"It is good to see you out and about, Weed," Father says as I finish lighting the candles and take my seat.

"My time beneath the ground is over," Weed replies simply. "I have come up now."

Father nods in approval. "There is room in the storeroom to make a bed for you; that is where you must sleep from now on."

"And there is a window there, too," I interject. "Every morning you will awaken to the sun."

Weed looks at me with gratitude. "Thank you for what I am about to receive," he says in a loud, strong voice. Father raises an eyebrow but does not comment, and I ladle the food onto each plate.

We eat. Father and I often share dinner in silence, but with Weed at the table the lack of conversation seems awkward. Father seems to feel so, too.

"Well," he remarks. "How did you two spend this lovely day?"

Weed's mouth is already full of food. "We took a walk, Father," I answer for us both. "To the stone circle and back."

"I imagine Jessamine explained the significance of the stone circle?"

Weed nods.

"We saw a stoat killing a rabbit," I interject. "It was quite vicious. And the rabbit made the most horrible sound—"

Father seems to not hear me; all his attention is fixed on Weed. "It must have been pleasant for you to be outdoors, after all those days in the cellar. Did you see any plants of interest?"

"They are all of interest," Weed says politely.

Father smiles. "Indeed. And what did you think of our gardens?"

Weed scarcely pauses before answering. "The gardens are very well tended. The soil is black and loamy and full of worms. The radishes were planted at just the right time; they will grow well. There is a clump of bee balm that will fare better if it is cut back and divided into two—no, three plants, that will give the most blooms, I think. And the marigold wants more sun and should be moved."

I can hardly swallow for surprise; it is uncanny how Weed noticed every detail during our walk.

Father pushes his food around his plate with the fork. "It seems Mr. Pratt was right about one thing; you do know a great deal about plants," he says finally. "Did you happen to pass by the apothecary garden?"

"The one that infests the northern slope?" Weed says calmly, shoving a chunk of lamb chop into his mouth. "The one that stinks of death?"

I nearly gasp—I know Father will be furious at this rude reply. Ought I to say something about the sudden illness that afflicted Weed when we approached the locked gate? Will Weed mention it?

But Father merely stares at Weed. If he is angry, he hides it well. He nods in the affirmative.

"That garden is locked, sir." Weed's voice is mild, but there is a trace of iron beneath.

"Yes, it is locked," Father says after a long pause, "and for good reason. Though I confess, I would be curious to know if you are familiar with the plants that grow within its walls. Over the years I have collected a great many unusual specimens."

Is Father going to relent? My fear is just as quickly replaced by hope. *Is he going to invite us into the apothecary garden at last?*

Weed gazes steadily at Father, his green eyes murky as a stagnant pool. "It is locked," he says, in an echo of Father's words, "and for good reason."

The vein on Father's forehead throbs once—twice—then brusquely he stands and pushes his chair away from the table.

"This was a fine dinner, Jessamine. Thank you for preparing it. Now I must get back to my work, as I know you must get back to yours." His voice is controlled, but the fingers of his right hand twitch as he speaks. "I bid you both good night."

Without waiting for a reply, Father exits the room. The meal he has just praised lies half eaten on his plate.

"Father never lingers at the table; that is his way," I explain to Weed, to hide my embarrassment at Father's abrupt exit. "But you may stay and eat as much as you like."

Weed nods. He has already devoured every scrap of his own food, but he reaches his hand across the table until it floats above Father's plate. It hovers there briefly, then delicately drops and seizes a lamb chop by the bone.

"A fine dinner, Jessamine." Once more he echoes Father's words. "This was a fine dinner. Thank you."

He eats the remains of Father's meal. I watch, filled with an unfamiliar feeling of contentment and think: *Jessamine, Jessamine, Jessamine.*

It is the first time he has spoken my name.

7

22nd April

So much to do, there is scarcely time to write
anything down. The garden grows as never before,
and I must work my hardest to keep up.
   I am glad Weed is here to help.

APRIL IS A MIRACLE, every year—between morning and evening I notice the garden change, as buds
burst open, petals unfurl, and last year's woody brown
stalks grow tall with new green shoots. But in all of

Northumberland, nothing grows as tall and handsome as Weed.

In scarcely more than a month, he has gained four inches. Now he stands taller than I do, and looks to be getting taller still. When he wears Father's trousers he no longer has to roll them up at the bottom. His limbs are slim and strong, like the branches of a willow.

His black hair is still wild, for that is the way it naturally grows. His dark eyebrows curve in two brooding crescents above his shockingly green eyes.

His mouth is changeable—sometimes wide and grinning, sometimes soft and full.

His teeth are white as snowdrops. His complexion, once so pale, is now tinged golden from the sun.

If I thought for a heartbeat that, even deep within the private corners of his own mind, Weed dissected and scrutinized *me* in just this way, piece by piece—*eye, lip, nose, cheek*—I would be mortified beyond all hope of recovery. But I mean no disrespect by it. It is because I am so used to observing and recording everything I see: the weather, the plants, the changes in the garden. Depicting that which interests me has become second nature, and nothing is as interesting to me as the time I spend with Weed. Thus I cannot help but try (and fail miserably, I fear!) to describe him in detail—as if he were some unusual plant Father might have brought home in his satchel.

I write about him by candlelight, while I am upstairs in my bedchamber and he lies sleeping in the storeroom below. The more I struggle to describe this unique being, the more it feels as if he were right here, next to me—is it foolish to be lonely for him when I know I will see him in the morning?

Sometimes it feels as if morning will never come.

Weed and I take long walks together nearly every day, once all our chores are done. He seems to know everything about how to make the garden thrive, though sometimes I find his advice curious. This morning he suggested that the rue plants would grow better if they were moved as far as possible from the lavender. When I asked why, he just laughed and said, "I do not know; perhaps they have had an argument." But I have learned to trust his advice, and the work is quick and enjoyable because of him.

When we walk he leads us far from the cottage. We wander until he announces, for no particular reason that I can see, that it is time to stop. Then he lies on his back on the ground and listens—to the birds, I suppose, or to the sound of the wind whistling through the leaves. Whole afternoons pass in this way.

Today is no different. We lie here, near to each other but not touching, and somehow my heart manages to feel full to bursting and light as air, all at the same time.

"You must think I am mad," he says, rolling on his side to look at me.

"Why would I think that?"

He does not answer right away, but the notion of madness causes my mind to recollect the strange accusations made by that awful Mr. Pratt on the day Weed first came to live with us. "I did not believe a word of Pratt's story, Weed," I say to reassure him. "I hope you have no fear on that account. I do not know what happened at the madhouse, but even a blind person could see that Tobias Pratt is not an honorable man."

Weed smiles. "All I meant was, mad to spend so much time just lying on the ground, listening."

"Oh!" I blush with embarrassment at the way I misunderstood his meaning. "I like resting here, too. It feels peaceful."

"And the music," he murmurs, settling back to face the sky. "The grass—the wind—makes such a beautiful song."

"I will sing to you," I say impulsively. If there were anyone present other than Weed I would never make such an offer, for I hardly know any songs. But there is an old ballad that Mama used to sing to me, and I can remember most of the tune, I think.

"Please do," Weed encourages, closing his eyes.

Propping myself up on an elbow, I take a breath and begin. It is a sad, strange song about a shepherd boy who lies sleeping in a meadow and is kissed by a passing girl to wake him, so his flock does not wander off. But she cannot rouse him, for the shepherd boy is not sleeping at all—he is dead.

I let the last note fade away. The moment is unexpectedly tender; the feeling both excites and frightens me. Without lifting himself from the ground, Weed turns his head until his gaze meets mine. His eyes are luminous, the same vivid green as the grass we now lie in.

I reach toward him, not because I choose to but because my limbs seem to have developed a will of their own. I long to touch his cheek, but I dare not. Instead, I pluck a yellow-headed dandelion from the tall grass next to his shoulder and offer it to him with mock gravity.

"Tell me, shepherd boy: How did you like my song?"

At the sight of the flower he jumps up, as if in a fury. He clenches his fists in front of his face and turns away.

96

"Enough," he says, in a voice full of bitterness and pain. "Let us go home."

Weed's mysterious grief hangs on us like a fog. As we walk home I ask more than once if he is angry about the song, or the flower, or Tobias Pratt. He says he is fine. I beg him to tell me if I have done something wrong. Again he assures me I have not. But he cannot smile, either, and will not look at me—oh, it is like a knife in my heart!

When we arrive at the cottage, Father is hurriedly packing his medical bag.

"A messenger just came, with an urgent summons. I must leave at once." He sounds deeply displeased.

"Are you going to London again?" I blurt.

Father continues throwing items into his satchel. "No. The patient is right here in Hulne Park, at the lumber mill. There was an accident—a man's foot is badly mangled. The idiots think I can save it by sprinkling a few rose petals on the poor fellow's head." He slams the bag shut. "For this I must interrupt my

97

research? Even if I had the skill of Hippocrates, what then? Could the wisdom of the ages stop a careless oaf from dropping an ax on his foot?"

Weed sucks in a long, raspy breath and runs out of the cottage. Moments later he comes back. His face is ashen, and he holds a small bundle of stems and leaves. Wordlessly he offers them to Father.

Father stares at the plants, bewildered. "Rue? Tansy? Chamomile? These are common roadside plants. What is all this for?"

"Make a poultice. It will prevent infection so the wound can heal," he says in a low voice. "For pain . . . use the poppy, mixed with valerian. No doubt the man is afraid; lavender and chamomile will soothe him." His voice drops to a whisper. "And—if it has to come off—"

"If the foot has to come off, it is the surgeon's problem, and whiskey is the only medicine those butchers use," Father growls. "Whiskey, and strong leather straps."

"No whiskey—use some belladonna—not too

much. Mix it with seeds of hemlock and black henbane. It will make him sleep."

"Sleep!" Father cries. "Through an amputation?
Impossible; it has been centuries since that formula
was lost—"

"Two berries only! I know you have some. The
man will sleep for a night and a day, and awaken when
the worst is over."

Father drops his bag and steps very close to Weed.
They are nearly the same height, but Father has twice
his bulk. My mouth goes dry; what will Father do?

"How do you know these things?" Father hisses
through his teeth. "Tell me, 'Doctor' Weed—where
did you steal your secret formulas from, eh?" His
hands rise; for a moment I fear he will seize Weed
and shake him.

Weed stares at him, his bottomless green eyes glit-
tering with defiance. "Go to the sawmill," he says. "No
time to waste." Then, letting the leaves fall through
his fingers to the floor, he turns and walks out of the
cottage.

I run to Father's side and take his arm. The vein in his forehead throbs and his lips are pressed into a furious white line.

"Father, do not be angry," I plead. "He is only trying to help." On hands and knees I gather up the torn leaves that have fallen at our feet and hold them out to Father.

Slowly Father regains control of himself. He takes the leaves from me, seizes his satchel, and starts for the door.

"Wait!" I run to Father's study and stretch high on tiptoe to grab the glass jar of belladonna berries from the shelf. Cradling the jar like a baby, I race back to the parlor, breathless.

"Here, Father—the belladonna—"

His temper explodes. "*Jessamine!* Have you lost your mind?"

"Take some with you, Father. In case the man needs them. Weed said two—two berries only—"

I struggle to get the lid off the jar. In doing so, I lose my grip—it starts to slip from my hand—

"No!" Father catches the jar before it falls and shatters. I snatch the jar from Father, pour two berries into my handkerchief, and tie them in a secure bundle.

"Take these, too, please, Father," I beg. "Do as Weed says. I know you will not regret it."

Cursing under his breath, Father takes the berries from me. He shoves them and the torn leaves roughly into his satchel and storms out of the cottage.

After Father goes, I find Weed in the herb garden, sitting very still among the plants. I bring him some water. He takes it with a look of gratitude but says nothing, and I have no choice but to leave him be. An hour goes by, then another. At times I swear I can hear him speaking quietly—but with whom?

Late this evening I walk through the house, candle in hand, to extinguish all the lamps. It only then that I notice the belladonna is still sitting out in the parlor. Carefully I secure the lid and return the jar to Father's study.

Before I put the jar back on the shelf, I hold my

candle next to it so that I may admire the black orbs within. The soft light flickers across their glossy skin, making the berries look strangely alive. They are dark, spherical, shining, deadly. Beautiful.

Like staring into the pupils of a murderess, I think.

8

23rd April

No word from Father.
   Weed is not speaking to me, either.
   What has happened to my family, my new and only friend? I am bereft.

WEED HAS BEEN OUTSIDE in the garden all night, and now it is morning. For the most part I have left him alone, though every now and then I look out my window to see if he is all right.

I may be mistaken, but it seems that he pays special attention to the plants from which he tore leaves yesterday to give to Father: the rue, tansy, poppy, chamomile, and lavender. He sits quietly by each one in turn. His lips scarcely move, but his expression is that of a person in deep conversation.

Seeing him out there fills me with dread. I am filled with questions that I am too afraid to ask.

If he is mad, I think, *at least it is a harmless kind of madness, to sit and talk to plants, as if they could hear one's words, and comprehend one's meaning, isn't it?*

The sun is low in the sky. Weed has not returned to the house, nor is he in the garden. I suppose he may have taken a walk by himself. The thought brings tears to my eyes, and I am instantly ashamed—foolish, spoiled Jessamine! Surely I can keep myself occupied for an afternoon without weeping like a baby.

In any case, I have had all day to think about what happened yesterday. I do not know how Weed knows the things he knows, or why he was so disturbed when

I picked the dandelion, or what he was doing in the garden last night. And I can well imagine how infuriating it is to Father that Weed refuses to reveal the source of his knowledge.

But one thing is clear: Father and Weed must become friends, for I cannot bear another incident of being torn between them like this. They are both too dear to me.

And too alike, I think, with their mysterious moods and closely guarded secrets.

They both are also very good at leaving me alone, it seems.

It is after dark when Father returns. His mood is calm, even serene. But it has always been thus with Father; his moods pass like little storms: a brief, violent bluster followed by tranquil skies.

"Did you save the man's foot?" Quickly I heat up some dinner in a skillet. I know Father must be hungry after his journey.

He nods. "They think I am a miracle worker,

though you and I know who truly deserves the credit. Where is Weed, Jessamine? I wish to speak to him. No doubt he is afraid to face me now, but he need not be. Can you persuade him to come see me?"

"I will try."

I was too proud and fearful to search for Weed earlier, but now that Father wants to reconcile I am prepared to wander all over the county in search of him. There is no need: Before I reach the footpath I find him lying on the ground, hidden among the plants of the dye garden. His hand rests lightly upon the bloodroot, almost as if he had been petting it.

Where have you been? Why have you not confided in me? How could you leave me alone all day with no companion but my own fears and unanswered questions? My thoughts are as tangled and thorny as a hedge of brambles, and I force them down, deep inside, so that I may speak calmly.

"Come inside, Weed," I say. "Father has returned; he wishes to speak to you."

Weed scowls and turns away.

"He saved the man's foot because of your advice. Don't you wish to know what happened?"

"This is how it was at the madhouse," Weed mutters. "I tried to help people who were sick. Then everyone became furious." He looks up at me, anger and confusion in his eyes. "I do not understand. Is it wrong to help?"

"No! Helping others is God's work. It is what we are put on earth to do." I hold out a hand, which he ignores. "Father is not angry with you, Weed. Do not misunderstand his strong feelings. It is only because he so passionately wishes to cure people who are in need, and he does not always know how."

Weed glances warily at the cottage. "Is that what he wishes to speak to me about?"

"I think so. Will you come?"

"Do you wish me to, Jessamine?"

He gazes upon me, then, and his emerald eyes seem to take me in from top to bottom. I feel so bared, my hands flutter to my dress to make sure it is still on. It is, but I am suddenly, exquisitely aware of how the currents of warm air move against my skin.

Weed rises to his feet. "Nature," he says softly, "makes so many beautiful things." He leans close to me, as if he would catch my scent. "But I did not know—until you—that nature could make a girl so beautiful."

His voice holds me in its tender spell. His eyes graze over my body without shyness—he takes me in as a landscape, a lush terrain of swells and valleys.

He leans forward, then. My heart thumps so strongly in my chest I am sure he must hear it. His face comes close, closer to mine—so close, a stray lock of his wild hair caresses my cheek.

I should move away. I do not. Instead, I close my eyes. My lips part and a sense of yearning fills me, a longing for something I cannot name. It is a force larger than myself that moves through me, ancient as the earth. There is no choice but to surrender.

He kisses me. His lips are petal soft against mine, his body strong and lithe as a poplar. He smells of rich, fertile earth.

After an eternity he releases me. Without waiting for my reaction, he turns and strides back to the cottage.

When I regain power over my limbs, I make my way back to the cottage in fits and starts, like a leaf tossed about by the wind. I hesitate at the door—am I even recognizable? The news must be written all over me, illustrated on my flesh. The moment Father lays eyes on me he will know I am transformed, and demand to know how, and why—oh, my lips burn, all the skin on my body burns! A tisane of lavender and hyssop would calm me, but I do not wish to be calmed!

I wish only for Weed, to see Weed again, to touch him, and I will, the moment I pass through the door of the cottage—

Weed stands in the parlor, shoulders hunched, staring down at the table, upon which Father's handkerchief lies. Father sits in his chair at the head of the table. Neither of them looks at me or says hello.

Father flips open the white linen, revealing the belladonna berries.

"As it turned out, I did not need the belladonna this time, Weed. Thanks to your poultice, the man's wounds started to heal cleanly, with no gangrene or fever."

Father covers the berries again and slips the handkerchief into his pocket.

"You have knowledge that can help people, Weed. That much is obvious. I wish to know where you acquired this knowledge, so that I may follow in your footsteps. But if you will not or cannot tell me, then at least teach me some of what you know."

Weed's eyes stay fixed on the table. "I have nothing to teach," he says in a low voice.

"Your humility is admirable, but of no use to anyone." Father rises from his chair and sits on the edge of the table, nearer to Weed. "It is time to be frank with each other. I value your knowledge, Weed. I admire it. I admit, I envy it. Think of it: belladonna, hemlock, black henbane—the lost formula for a twilight sleep! A sleep so profound a man would not feel his own limb being cut off."

110

He looks at Weed as if expecting some reaction, but there is none. Father seems to interpret this as interest, or at least a willingness to hear more, for he goes on.

"Behind the walls of my apothecary garden are other rare and even more dangerous plants. Many I acquired without fully understanding their uses—perhaps I found a name mentioned in some obscure, ancient medical text, or came upon an old cure related by a beggar who claimed to have heard it from an ancient witch woman he met once. Based upon such vague hints and clues, and often following nothing more than my own blind instincts, I have bought and traded plants from all over the world. The most powerful ones live behind that locked gate."

Weed's face is impassive; his attention seems to have turned inward. Undaunted, Father continues.

"I have gone to great pains to try to learn the uses and properties of these plants. I have spent countless hours in pursuit of this knowledge. You could save me a great deal of time and effort, if you would only speak. . . ." Father stops himself. He stands, and spreads his hands before Weed in a gesture of supplication. "Weed. I wish to take you into the apothecary garden. I want you to look at the plants that grow there and tell me what you know of them."

Weed recoils as if struck. "No!" he exclaims. "That garden is dangerous. Dangerous for me—dangerous for everyone."

Father scowls, puzzled. So far he has not even acknowledged my presence, but I step forward now to explain. "Father, even walking near the apothecary garden made Weed feel very ill. Perhaps he is afraid that some harm may come to him if he enters it."

To my amazement, Father places his hands gently on Weed's shoulders. He speaks warmly, as a father would speak to a beloved son. "It may be a difficult thing I ask of you, but I implore you to at least try. Remember, it is not for me I ask. Think of the people who might be cured."

I have never seen Father speak so humbly, so earnestly, to anyone.

112

Weed turns his gaze to me. Our eyes meet, and though the table is between us, it is suddenly as if our kiss never ended. Even now I am standing in his arms, our lips pressed together, breathing his clean, sun-warmed scent.

"Jessamine." His voice warms me, deep inside. "What would you have me do?"

Father looks at me too, waiting for my answer. I know full well what he would have me say. Oh, I am torn! Heaven knows how much and for how long I have yearned to go inside that forbidden garden—but does Weed know something I do not?

Think of the people who might be cured. . . .

That is what Father said, but in my heart I hear:

It is too late to save Mama . . . but think of the others. . . .

"Father will not allow any harm to come to you," I say firmly. "You must trust him fully, just as you trust me. And I will come into the garden, too," I add, looking hard at Father, "and stay by your side every minute, Weed."

Father nods his assent.

"As you wish." Weed sounds reluctant but resigned, as if a long-dreaded fate he knows he cannot escape has finally come to pass. "Tomorrow it is, then."

With no warning, Father turns and hugs me, tightly, as if I were a child. I cannot remember the last time he has done that. I know it has been years.

"Into the garden we go, Jessamine," he murmurs into my hair. "It is time."

9

24th April

The weather is fair and mild.

Father says I am not permitted to write about what happens today. The contents of the apothecary garden must remain secret.

Did I mention that the weather is fair?

THE KEY TO THE APOTHECARY GARDEN hangs on a large circular key ring that I have never seen before. Father slips it out of his pocket with practiced familiarity.

Weed and I stand behind him. The morning air promises a warm day, but Weed seems frozen. I imagine he has steeled himself against whatever ill effects he fears the garden may have on him by cultivating a cold, blank exterior. How odd it is to stand so close to him and see no flicker of affection, no sign of our closeness of yesterday!

Soon, I think. *Soon we will be alone again, and the truth can finally be spoken.*

Father slips the key in the keyhole and turns it, until the lock falls open with a soft click. He shakes loose the heavy chain and lets it slip to the ground. In answer to a gentle push, the tall black gate swings open on smooth, silent hinges.

At last! I long to whoop in celebration, but I dare not. Something more somber and dangerous is at stake. Weed stands near me, his face impassive.

"Come inside; don't be afraid." Father gestures for us to follow.

My high spirits give me the courage to tease Father. "All right, but aren't you going to tell us not to touch anything?"

He smiles faintly. "I assumed you knew that by now."

As we step inside, the temperature of the air itself seems to change, as if a great cloud suddenly blotted out the sun. Weed shudders, but he does not hang back, and together we proceed.

Excitement courses through my every nerve. Is it because Weed is near me, or is it because, finally, after years of waiting, I stand inside the forbidden garden? Is the thrill of one any different than the thrill of the other? I cannot tell. He is with me, the garden is before me; my heart quickens with the rightness of it all.

And yet, as I look about, I am forced to admit: On its surface, the apothecary garden is not so very different from any other garden. There is the smell of rich earth, the green plants growing quietly in their beds, the soft hum of bees making their rounds.

Father walks ahead of us. He too seems charged with excitement; there is a spring in his step I do not often see. "My aim is to keep the plant families together as best I can, based on scientific principles," he explains. "Weed, are you familiar with the work of Carl Linnaeus? His *Systema Naturae* describes a classification system for all growing things."

Weed's eyes dart everywhere, probing every corner. "Unless he visited the madhouse, I never met him," he replies.

Father allows himself a wry smile. "Some consider him to be the greatest botanist of the century. I find his work useful, though no doubt future generations will call it primitive. I can instruct you in it if you like." He sweeps his hand around. "Bear in mind that what I have done here is, at best, an approximation of a true botanical garden, but that is because of the unusual nature of my collection. There are many plants here that have been collected from the farthest parts of the globe. Despite all my research, my knowledge of the relationships between them is scanty. Perhaps you will be able to enlighten me on that account, Weed."

Father does not wait for an answer. "Let us start our walk here, along the east wall. These are plants you may be familiar with. Some are native to England, and some were brought over from the American colonies a century ago—the United States of America, I suppose I ought to call it now. This plant, for example. Do you recognize it?"

"Angel's trumpet," Weed breathes. "A plant of many dreams."

Father looks at him sharply. "Dreams, yes—some might say hallucinations. Angel's trumpet, also known as datura. They say the name 'datura' comes from a Hindu word meaning 'thorn apple'—but perhaps you already knew that."

Weed presses his forehead with both palms and squeezes his eyes shut. Does he not know, or is he trying to rid himself of what knowledge he has?

"A craggy old fellow I met at the St. James fair told me that tidbit of lore," Father continues. "He specialized in plants of the Orient, and claimed to be a survivor of one of Captain Cook's expeditions. I suspect he was

119

lying about that, but the specimens he offered were quite rare. And the prices he charged were exorbitant, I must say."

Father continues to stroll as he talks. He seems fully at ease here inside his locked garden—more at ease than I have ever seen him, in fact. "This is henbane. And this is poison hemlock. A painless death, but a particularly cruel one, don't you think?"

"From the feet it begins," Weed intones.

Father nods. "Death starts from the feet and travels upward, until it reaches the heart and finally kills you, and the whole time you are fully aware of what is happening. They say it took poor Socrates twelve hours to die. Ah, here is a favorite of mine: wormwood, the ingredient that gives absinthe its peculiarly intoxicating properties." Father waves me closer. "Take a good look at the white bryony, Jessamine. It is all too easy to mistake its roots for parsnip. That would be the last bowl of soup any of us would ever enjoy."

We follow Father from plant to plant. "Bittersweet,"

120

he points out, "and adder's root, and mandrake. And this potent specimen is called oleander—"

Suddenly Weed clutches his head in pain. "No!" he cries. "These are not plants to heal the sick. These are poison! All of them . . . poison . . ."

Something twists inside my chest. Is it true? I knew these plants were dangerous if misused, Father always told me that—but is Father's private, closely guarded collection of plants really nothing more than a poison garden? A locked armory of deadly, living weapons? For what purpose would he, or anyone, create such a wicked place?

"You must know it is not as simple as that, Weed," Father says smoothly. "The plant that can kill can also cure, if only one has the knowledge to use it properly. That is why it is so important—so very important— that you tell me what you know."

Weed shakes his head violently back and forth, as if he would cast out some deeply embedded pain.

"Are you all right?" I cry out, but as I reach toward him I lose my balance and stumble into a nearby garden bed. My arm brushes against what looks like a nettle. It feels like a thousand pins plunging into my flesh. Within seconds, a tiger's striping of scarlet welts begins to rise and scroll around my skin.

Father does not even turn around. "Do be careful, Jessamine," he says casually, walking on. "I paid a great deal of money for some of these plants."

I cradle my wounded arm. The burning sensation forces tears into my eyes. Vivid, puffy stripes rise and spread with shocking speed. "A dock leaf will take way the sting," I tell Weed with forced calm, though I feel suddenly light-headed. "I'm sure we will find one on the walk home."

"A dock leaf might, if that were an ordinary nettle." Weed closes his eyes, then walks in staggering zigzags until he reaches a small group of plants near the southern fence. Dizzily I scurry after him.

"Weed," I whisper hoarsely. "Please, do not touch anything. Father will be furious—"

Ignoring my objections, he bends down and tears a leaf from a low, inconspicuous shrub, then stands and rubs it on my skin. The worst of the pain sub-sides at once, and the sharp pinpricks turn to a dull throbbing.

Father has wandered far ahead of us; now he turns. "Come along, you two, what is holding you back?" A glance from Weed instructs me to say nothing. I draw my shawl close around my arm to cover the welts, which are already starting to recede.

Father calls again: "Make haste, Jessamine. I want you to see this."

I glance behind me. Weed's lips are pale and moving rapidly, as if he were reciting some desperate prayer. *Please, let Father not see him acting so oddly*, I think.

Ahead, Father beckons. Obediently I go to him. He steps aside with a smile.

"Look—here are some old friends of yours."

Before me are the belladonna sprouts. Each one is nearly a foot tall now, delicate and lanky. They sway in unison with the breeze, like a company of dancers.

The sight of them makes me forget everything

else: the fading throb in my arm, Weed's bizarre behavior behind me on the path, Father's strange, cool indifference—

"My belladonna seeds!" I exclaim. "Look how well they are growing. Weed, come see."

I kneel down to get a better look at the infant shoots. Truly, it is a miracle, the way a tiny nubbin of a seed can so quickly transform into lush green growth.

"Isn't it amazing?" I say to Weed, who now stands next to me. He looks ashen and preoccupied. I keep my voice merry and my arm hidden beneath my shawl, so Father will not suspect anything is amiss. "Before the season is over these plants will be nearly as tall as I am."

Playfully, I tease the little plants with the tip of a stick I find on the ground. "Hello, lovely girls. I wonder if you remember me? Jessamine, who bathed you so tenderly, and cared for you every day before you were born?"

With sudden violence Weed seizes the stick and

snaps it in two. He looks at me, as if astonished by his own act. Then he groans and collapses to the ground.

Father and I carry a half-conscious Weed back to the cottage. He feels impossibly heavy; with each step it is as if we are pulling him from the earth.

"Did you see him touch any of the plants?" Father grunts. "Did he taste anything? Smell anything?"

We will be banned forever from the garden now, I think, but for Weed's sake I tell the truth. "He did, Father, but only to help me. When I fell into that nettle plant, he tore a leaf from something to ease the burning." I drop my shawl and hold up my arm to show him. The red welts have already faded, and the skin is cool and flat, with only faint pink streaks to show where I was hurt.

"Which plant? *Which plant did he touch?*"

"I don't know!" The look on Father's face is terrifying; for an awful moment I cannot tell if he is upset because Weed is ill, or because he had the nerve to tear a leaf from one of Father's precious plants—or because Father himself did not know which plant cured the nettle sting.

With Weed slung over his shoulder, Father opens the cottage door with a violent kick and marches straight up the stairs to my bedchamber.

"Can you help him?" I plead.

Father lets Weed slide off his shoulder and onto the bed, then walks around the room and opens all the windows fully. "If he did not ingest any of the leaves, the fresh air will revive him soon enough. And if he did, he is worse than a fool, for he must have known exactly what would happen."

He turns and looks down at his patient. Weed's breaths come evenly, and his eyes flutter back and forth beneath closed lids.

"He dreams. That is a good sign." Father takes a light blanket and places it over Weed's frame. "If only I could look through some enchanted lens that would let me observe those dreams," he murmurs. "They might reveal much."

I too long for such an enchanted lens. *Do you dream of me, Weed?* I wonder. *Do you dream of our kiss, as I do? Or was it only a moment's fancy, already forgotten?*

Father's penetrating gaze finds me and pins me to the spot. "I am more sure of it than ever, Jessamine. Somehow this silent, unschooled boy knows more than I do about the very plants I have made my life's work. But how? Has he revealed anything to you? You must not keep it from me if so."

"I do not know what Weed knows, or how," I say earnestly. "I wish I did."

Father stares at me until I have to look away.

I do not think he believes me.

I spend the night dozing in a chair I drag up to my bedchamber from the parlor. My sleep is so light and broken that I dream all night long. They are strange dreams of icy water, swirling about my ears—

I am a mere speck tossed about in a turbulent sea, while a smiling giantess empties and refills the ocean beds with

127

rushing, foam-flecked tides, again and again and again—

It is nearly dawn before Weed begins to stir. At once I am at his bedside. His eyes do not open, but he breathes a single word:

"Jessamine."

My heart swells until it hurts. What is this feeling, this deep ache that contains both pain and joy? Is it some leftover poison from that strange nettle? Is it love?

"I am here, Weed." I lift his hair back off his forehead. "I was so frightened! What happened to you in the garden? Was it anything to do with that leaf you picked?"

He shakes his head. "The voices are strong there. So strong, so cruel. So beautiful. They want me to stay."

"What voices? Who wants you to stay?"

He looks at me with those fathomless green eyes. "Jessamine," he whispers, so softly his words seem to enter my ears like the sound of a breeze in the meadow. "I am not like other people. I ought not to speak of these things."

128

My mind whirls—there is so much about Weed I do not know. So much I could ask, and should ask— but I am afraid.

Surely it would be better not to know. . . .

But I must be braver than that. "I touched the belladonna plants with a stick," I say, in a trembling voice. "And then you cried out."

His eyes widen into two green marbles, swirls of liquid emerald enclosed within perfect spheres. The early morning sun renders their color translucent, like the licorice-scented absinthe Father drips into his water glass, one intoxicating spoonful at a time.

I take Weed's hand in both of my own. "Can you at least tell me why you collapsed in the apothecary garden?" I plead. "These voices of yours—to whom do they belong?"

The curtains billow inward from the window. The fragrant spring air caresses us both. I lean forward until my face is a handsbreadth from his. I close my eyes and imagine brushing my lips against his, again and again.

"Tell me what you know," I whisper. "Show me what you see."

"I wish I could." He turns his face away. "But I cannot."

The kiss dies on my lips.

10

15th May

*No work is permitted today. It is a holiday! I have
declared it to be Weed's birthday.*

*He is still puzzled by the notion, so I suppose
I will have to explain it to him. In any case, it is a
pleasant excuse to skip chores and have a picnic.*

WEED IS SEVENTEEN NOW, more or less.

After the incident with the dandelion I know
better than to weave daisy chains and drape them

around his neck in honor of the day (or the week, or the month—birthday calculations are no more than a guess, in Weed's case).

I ask him if I may give him a small gift. I do not wish to embarrass him or be intrusive, but I know he is not likely to have received many birthday presents in his life. I would like to remedy that a little, if I could.

"You may, if you like" is his shrugged reply. "If it would make you happy."

"It would, but it is more important that it make *you* happy. That is the whole point of a present. Is there something in particular you would enjoy?"

He smiles and says only, "Good soil, sun, and rain. What more does one need in the spring?"

Not willing to take dirt, sun, and rain for an answer, I secretly begin to knit him a scarf, in shades of green and brown, interwoven with flecks of daffodil yellow. Since it will not be finished for a few days yet, I also choose a book I think Weed might find interesting, from among some of Father's recent purchases in London.

132

I bake a tray of small seedcakes with a honey glaze. I wrap them in linen napkins and place them in a basket to take with us on our afternoon ramble, along with a bottle of cider, the book I plan to give as a gift, and some paper and charcoal pencils for sketching in case the mood strikes us.

Father is gone for the day on some explorations of his own. I am glad of his absence, to be truthful—he watches Weed too carefully now, ever since our trip to the walled garden and Weed's subsequent brief illness. He hovers too close, asks too many questions. Certainly that is no way to spend a birthday!

Weed waits, somewhat bemused, as I prepare the basket. Finally we head off. Together we walk a long way, until we find a pleasant grassy knoll where we can sit and unpack our lunch. The air is sweet and buzzes with the hum of insect wings.

"Don't you envy the bees—the way they can crawl right inside the flower?" I say, swatting some of the eager intruders away from the sticky glaze on the cakes. "It must be so soft and sweet smelling in there among the petals. I wonder if it tickles?"

"I have reason to think it does," Weed replies contentedly, gazing up at the sky. "The bees have a very close knowledge of the blossom."

"More so than even the greatest botanists." I pour two small glasses of cider and hand one to Weed, who murmurs his customary words of grace. "I used to think I would like to be a botanist someday, but Father forbids me to study. Luckily he always leaves stacks of books by his chair in the parlor. I often sneak one or two when he is not looking."

"That is dishonest," Weed says, not sounding particularly disturbed.

I take a nibble of seedcake, still warm from the hearth. "I have no choice. Father says, 'Anyone who thinks botany is a fit profession for a lady does not know much about plants.'"

Weed rolls on his side and smiles. "It sounds as if he believes there is something sinful about horticulture."

"Oh, but there is!" I remove the book from the bottom of the basket and open it. "This volume describes the classification system of the Swedish botanist Carl Linnaeus, whom Father mentioned when we walked together in the apothecary garden. If it pleases you, you may have it as a birthday present."

"Thank you," Weed says. "I may not understand it, but thank you."

I cannot help but laugh. "I hope you will understand it! Linnaeus says the plants get married and make new plant families, and then those families intermarry and create the species, and then the species intermarry and produce the varieties. You can see why Father would object."

"I suppose," says Weed. "But at least they were all legally wed." He rolls over then and asks me quite bluntly, "Will you marry someday, Jessamine?"

"Of course," I blurt, suddenly flustered. "Or—I don't know. I suppose I will, but one must first—that is to say, a suitable person would have to propose to me, and I would have to accept, and my father would have to approve, also." *Does he not even remember how we kissed?* I think, bewildered. Surely it is not my place to remind him!

"What is suitable?" he asks, all innocence.

"Weed, your questions are so bold today!" I make myself sound cross to conceal how confused I feel. "A suitable person would be someone whom I cared for, who cared for me, and was kind and understanding and able to make a good home with me."

"Was I wrong to kiss you if I am not suitable, then?"

His words have the impact of a blow. "You were certainly wrong to kiss me," I exclaim, "if you meant nothing by it!"

"Jessamine! I am sorry. Please—don't cry!"

But it is too late; my feelings spill out in a rain of tears. "What does that mean, that you are not suitable?" I gasp out between sobs. "Do you not care for me at all, then?"

"Of course I care for you!" he exclaims. Even through my own tears I can see there is real pain in his eyes, and surprise as well. "And do you care for me also?"

"Yes," I confess. "Yes, I do."

But I cannot speak more, because he kisses me again, differently this time—this kiss is no tender question, but the luxurious, entitled kiss of one who now knows his feelings are returned. The sweet taste of seedcakes and cider mingles on our lips. My quickening heart fills my ears with a rushing sound, like the wind in the grass, like the sea.

After what seems a blissful aeon, he pulls away and gazes upon me. His look is so full of innocence, like a wild thing—utterly guileless and full of mystery at the same time.

"Weed," I say, now smiling through my tears. "You are really not like anyone else I have ever met."

"I know," he says darkly. "I know."

The next morning brings a fresh surprise: Father needs us to run an errand in Alnwick—not just in the town, but at the castle itself. I am excited, as I have only been inside the castle gates a few times in my life.

Weed is unimpressed by all that but is content to

escort me on the journey. I briefly wonder if Father had considered sending Weed alone, but perhaps Father does not fully trust Weed with his precious medicines just yet—for that is our errand, to deliver a packet of fever remedy to one of the duke's servants.

It is a little more than an hour's walk to Alnwick, a modest distance to experienced wanderers like Weed and myself. But there is a storm brewing low in the eastern sky, blowing in from the sea. We set off early at a brisk pace, in the hopes of returning home before it breaks. When we arrive at the crossroads, Weed stops.

"North, south, east, west," he says quietly. "Four directions in which to run away. But now all I feel is how much I would like to stay at Hulne Abbey, with you."

"I am glad," I say. The depth of my joy is almost too much to express.

"It seems I have put down roots," Weed adds as we turn down the southern road.

138

The closer we get to Alnwick, the more fellow travelers we encounter.

"It must be market day," I observe, pulling my cloak around my head. "Too bad we cannot stay."

"Why not?"

I shrug. "Father always taught me to avoid mingling with the townspeople. When I was young, he worried that they might trick me into revealing some of his hard-earned knowledge. Now I suppose he worries that they might think me a witch."

We cut quickly through the crowds, picking our way over cobblestone streets to Bailiffgate, through which the road to the castle passes.

"Father took me into the keep once or twice, many years ago, not long after Mama died and there was no one to watch me at Hulne Abbey," I explain. "He comes to use the duke's library."

"Why is he permitted to do that?"

"It is in payment for his services. Years ago the duke offered him the old chapel to live in and a yearly income, if the people of Alnwick might have free use of his medical skills. Father replied that, since the chapel was only a ruin, he had no qualms about taking it off the duke's hands, as long as he would be permitted to plant gardens all around, but he would rather have the run of the library than a salary. Oh, Weed, there it is—look."

The road has led us to the bottom of a wildflower-strewn hill. Above and before us is the ancient, terrifying grandeur of Alnwick Castle.

"Yes," Weed murmurs, his eyes still fixed on the ground. "It is beautiful—very beautiful indeed."

According to Father's instructions, the fever remedy is to be delivered to "Mrs. S. Flume, Cook." We gain entry by showing the guard the parcel and our letter of introduction from Father, which has the duke's seal on it. Nodding, the guard directs us to the kitchen entrance, which is to the left and down a steep stone stairway.

Underground, it is like a colony of ants, with servants racing back and forth through a maze of tunnels that lead to every corner of the castle. The servants push wheeled carts through the tunnels at a break-neck pace; Weed and I must press ourselves flat against the wall to avoid being run over. The only light in the tunnels comes from above, through small circular windows made of thick glass set directly in the ground above our heads, like portholes in a capsized ship.

"Pardon me," I shout above the clatter of wheels and dishes to a passing serving man. "We have a parcel for Mrs. Flume. It is urgent."

The man can barely hear us. "Who d' ye want?"

"Mrs. S. Flume!"

"Susannah Flume, did you say? She's not here, she's . . ."

His explanation gets lost in the din. Through gestures I signal that I cannot understand, and he motions for us to follow him. He leads us down long tunnels, past the smoky, blazing hot kitchen. Sweaty, bare-armed cooks and scullery maids chop, peel, stir, and keep themselves from passing out by drinking endless pints of small ale.

We keep going, through more winding tunnels and up a narrow stair that releases us back into the sunlight. We clamber down a grassy slope dotted with sheep until we reach the spot where an arched stone bridge spans the river Aln. Halfway across the bridge a great stone lion, the emblem of the duke's family, stands guard.

"There's the woman you seek," the man says. "That child of hers couldn't even get a proper burial—anyone dies these days, they say it's the plague." He gestures ahead. "That's all the funeral the poor thing'll have."

On the bank of the river, a small group of people surround a weeping woman. At her feet is a large basket of wildflowers, picked from the abundance of the meadow. One by one, the mourners toss the flower stalks into the water. They float sadly on the current until they disappear around the curve of the river.

One of the party, a girl in a rough linen apron, approaches us.

"Are you relatives?" she asks in a quivering voice.

"I am Jessamine Luxton," I say quickly. "My father

is Thomas Luxton, the apothecary. A fever remedy was sent for; we came to deliver it."

"You are good to come, Miss Luxton, and you, too, sir." The girl curtsies to Weed. "You are very kind to come all this way. Tell your father—tell him we're very grateful." She can say no more, and someone leads her away.

Weed looks at me blankly, uncomprehending.

"We are too late," I say, my eyes filling with tears.

The man who led us here nods. "Aye, miss. The child died this morning."

"I am so sorry. Father only got word yesterday."

"The fever came on too fast. Poor bairn."

A fresh group of mourners arrives over the bridge, bearing more baskets of flowers.

Weed falls to his knees. "No!" he cries, reaching for the baskets. "No!"

The man lays a rough hand on Weed's shoulder. "God gives 'em and God takes 'em away," he says comfortingly. "Even a short time on this earth is a blessing, I reckon—but for those of us what get left behind, sometimes it feels too hard to bear, don't I know it, son."

"Such needless killing," Weed murmurs as he touches one of the blooms. "They have no power to help anyone now." He covers his face with his hands.

Everyone thinks he is despondent over the dead child, but I see the way one hand lingers on the basket. My grief curdles into icy rage.

"What kind of freak are you?" I hiss in his ear. Then I turn and race back over the bridge. I cannot take the shortcut beneath the castle this time, for I know I will never find my way through those tunnels alone. I must run the long way around, through the muddy pastures that surround the outer bailey until I find my way back to the road.

I am through Bailiffgate and halfway down Market Street again before Weed catches up with me. He chases after me, calling my name, begging me to stop and listen. But I plug my ears with anger and hurt. I am furious at him, and at myself for my confusion, too— *This is Weed you run from, the same Weed you care for so much—how could you be so drawn to one so heartless? Yes, despite everything you still long for him to hold you, kiss you, even now you long for it—*

He catches me and seizes my arm. His grip is hard. I cry out in pain.

"Forgive me—you must forgive me, Jessamine! Try to understand. I know I seem cold, or freakish—but I do not know how to feel what you feel—you will have to teach me—"

"I think you have no feelings at all!" I cry. "Not real ones, anyway. The suffering of a daisy reduces you to tears. But a child—a dead child—dear God, Weed, you are monstrous!"

He flinches as if slapped.

"I am not monstrous," he whispers hoarsely. "But I am different from you, Jessamine. Different from everyone. I see things—I hear things—"

"So do I! I see you knowing things you cannot possibly know. I hear you speaking when no one is near. I feel you keeping secrets from me, even as you hold me in your arms." I try and fail to pull away from him. "I cannot bear it anymore! Tell me what you are, Weed, or be gone from my life."

He releases his grip and stands before me. A gust of wind catches his hair, and the first raindrops begin to fall from darkening skies. "All right," he says after a moment. "I will tell you what you wish to know. Tomorrow at daybreak I will take you to the meadows. There you shall know everything."

He glances up at the gray sky. "And then you will truly hate me for a monster," he adds, as he walks ahead of me, into the storm.

11

WE LEAVE THE COTTAGE SILENTLY, by dawn's
light. Father is still asleep. If he rises to find us gone,
will he think something ill?

The thought comes to me unbidden: *It does not
matter what Father thinks.*

Weed does not say where he leads me, but except
for the early hour, the walk is our familiar one. We
arrive at a not-too-distant meadow and lower ourselves onto the dew-soaked grass. Indifferent to the
wet, Weed stretches out on his back, his whole form
pressed against the earth.

I take my place next to him. Goose bumps rise on my flesh from the cold earth, and from my anticipation, too. What horrifying truth does he intend to show me? Ought I to be afraid? Perhaps, but my sense of excitement far outweighs any fear.

Finally Weed speaks.

"As we walked here, did you see the grass?" he says. "The trees? The dandelions? The fields of oilseed?"

"I did."

"Can you hear them?"

I think he means the soft, oceanic rushing, the wind in the grass, the fluttering of leaves. "Yes," I reply. "When there is a breeze, I hear them."

"But do you hear them in words?"

"No, of course not."

"I do," he says quietly. "I hear everything they say."

"I do not understand—"

He holds a hand up, to silence me, and raises himself up on one elbow. "Look over there, in the shade beneath the hedgerow. Do you see the mat of broad leaves against the ground, the fresh green spike that will soon be covered with flowers?"

"It is foxglove," I say, also rising. "Father sends me out to gather the leaves sometimes. They are useful to him in his work, and the wild ones are better than what we might grow in the garden."

"They do not like to be tamed, that is true." He cocks his head as if listening. "And they are very vain about their flowers when in bloom." He flinches a little, as if being scolded. "But they have every right to be, as they have just reminded me."

Is Weed playing a game with me? I turn so that I can see his face. "What are the foxgloves saying now?"

He meets my gaze with reluctance. "They say they know you. You have spent many hours lying near them, in the arms of the meadow grass. They say they hope I am not jealous. And they think you are very pretty. Too pretty." He listens again. "They are being rude now. It seems they are the jealous ones. You should not pick their leaves any time soon; they would be sure to give you a rash."

He is mad, I think in despair. *This is his monstrous*

*secret. Unless—unless what he says is true—and if it is,
dear God, what would Father make of such a power—to
gain knowledge directly from nature itself?* But I cannot
imagine any further. Instead, I will myself to respond
calmly, as if conversing with clumps of leaves were a
perfectly normal thing to do.

"Is it the same for all the plants?" I ask, keeping
my voice steady.

"Each one is different," he explains hesitantly. "If
I concentrate I can hear most of them—sometimes
only in cries and moans, or as a constant buzz of chatter. But it is the plants that have special powers to cure
whom I hear most clearly. They have always sought
me out, for as long as I can remember."

"Sought you out?" I exclaim. "How can a plant
seek you out?"

"They speak to me. They have to—for if no one
of human birth knew of their powers, how could they
make use of them? They need me," he explains simply.
"They chose me because I can hear them—or perhaps
I can hear them because they chose me; I have never

150

truly understood how it came to pass. But it did."

The silence between us grows heavy with the weight of Weed's revelation. I do not know what to think, or to say—can such a tale possibly be true?

After a moment he continues. "I was perhaps four or five before I realized that not everyone could hear what I heard. At first I was thought a strange, silent child with too much imagination. Later people started to think I was possessed, even dangerous. I learned to hide my gift. But it is difficult. Maddening, often. The voices are always there: humming, talking, singing, teasing, warning. There are times when I must get away from it, or I fear I will lose my mind." He smiles wryly. "The plants themselves gave me a cure for that: They taught me to bury myself when I need to regain my strength. It is what they do—return to the ground, rest, and begin again."

Suddenly I understand. "As you did when you first came here, by hiding in the cellar?" I ask.

"Yes." He rolls on his back, facing the sky. "One of the many times I ran away from the friar, I made my way to the docks and stowed away on a ship. I thought that if I went far out to the middle of the sea, I would be free of all those voices. But I was wrong. Even the oceans are full of growing things, did you know that? Some are so tiny you can scarcely see them, but they mass together in great blankets of green that float on top of the waves. They droned like bees, all the time. It was deafening. It nearly drove me mad." Abruptly he sits up. "Jessamine, do you believe me?"

I waver. What he describes is impossible, beyond belief—but have I not also sometimes thought I heard whispers in the rustling of leaves, or felt the calm strength of the trees in the forest? And he is Weed. He is not like anyone else, and what is impossible for others need not be impossible for him.

"I do believe you," I say.

He gazes at me steadily, probingly. To be one of a kind, to be ceaselessly addressed by voices that no one else can hear—I thought I understood loneliness, but now I realize I can scarcely begin to imagine the depth of his.

"And what of the plants in the poison garden?" I ask suddenly. "They are different, aren't they? Is that why they sickened you?"

He pauses and looks away. "Yes. They are powerful. Heartless. They wish to possess."

"Possess what?"

"Me. You. Everyone. That is their nature." A crease of disquiet snakes across his brow. "Your father plays with fire to gather them together like that. They are too clever. They form alliances. They develop—ambitions."

He looks so solemn I wish to soothe his fears. "You worry too much, I am sure," I say lightly. "After all, they are still rooted in the ground, are they not? They cannot pull themselves up and march around wreaking havoc, like an invading army."

"Maybe," he says, though he sounds unsure. "I have not met their like before; that is all. It disturbs me." He gestures around. "And not only me. The forests, the fields, the moss that grows on the rocks—none of them are happy about that garden. Nature would have kept those plants safely apart, scattered over the continents, separated by oceans. But your father has summoned them from the corners of the earth and locked them together, side by side, hidden behind walls, where they can grow in secret. It is wrong, Jessamine—I fear it is dangerous—"

"Promise me, then," I interrupt, for he is growing agitated. "Promise that you will never go in that awful place again. If it disturbs you so, then no good can come of it."

"I promise."

We fall silent. The morning has arrived in earnest now. One can almost hear the hiss of steam rising from the grass as the dew vanishes into the air.

I look around. Meadow, trees, hedgerows, patches of wildflowers here and there. I close my eyes and listen. Leaves rustling in the breeze. Birds singing. My own breath, rising and falling. Nothing else.

"You are right, Jessamine," Weed exclaims with sudden bitterness. "I am a freak."

"No!" I reach for him. "Forgive me, Weed, I

154

never should have spoken those words. I was angry because I did not know the truth. You have a gift. A precious gift."

"You are the first person to think so." There is both sadness and anger in his voice.

"Who else have you told?" I ask, suddenly fearful.

"I told Friar Bartholomew; I was only a child and knew no better. He did not believe me. He pitied me, I think, as a half-wit, and now he is dead in any case."

"But you did give something to Pratt's patients, did you not?" I press. "And what about the villagers?"

"I was foolish to try to help." His fingers play lightly in the grass. "But I hated Pratt, and wanted to teach him a lesson. And the plants asked me to do it. They want to make use of their talents—as we do."

He pauses for a moment. "I know now it was wrong to put anything in the well. But at the time, the villagers were not as real to me as—all this." His gaze encompasses the green growing things that surround us. "You have already taught me so much, Jessamine. Your grief yesterday at the castle, the grief of the others, of that poor mother—it was something I did not know before." He takes my hands. "I too would weep for the child now. I promise you, I would."

A soft smile lights up his face. "Before I met you, Jessamine, I never thought any human soul could understand. If you truly believe me, and are not afraid—*that* is the true gift, Jessamine. *You* are a gift."

"Weed, I will keep your secret as if my very life depends on it." My heart flails wildly in my chest, and I reach for him to steady myself. He takes my hands in his own, lifts them to his lips, and kisses them.

"I trust that you will." Still holding my hands to his lips, he murmurs, "I know your father already suspects something."

The heat of his breath burns my skin. *Here is where the road divides*, I think. Where does my loyalty lie? It does not take me even a single heartbeat to decide.

"I will not tell Father. I promise."

Right away I wish to explain myself, to justify my decision to lie: *Father is a good man, but knowing of*

156

your gift would drive him mad with envy. It would be too much for him to bear.

Weed requires no explanation. He releases my hands and draws me close to him. Now there is no turning back. The architect of my future has been switched, from father to lover. But is this not precisely what nature intends? There is a time for growth, and a time for blossoming. Father, of all people, should understand that. I fear he will not, though.

I skim my fingertips around Weed's face as if I were blind. I trace the curved dark eyebrows, the firm cheekbone underneath the petal-soft skin. My lips move toward his as a bee to a flower, eager to taste.

We kiss, and kiss again. Dizzy, I lean against the earth, yet I fly.

12

22nd May

The air is perfumed with spring. The sun warms the skin and melts the heart, and everything grows with abandon. Roots stretch deep in the earth to satisfy their thirst. Stalks race upward, propelled by joy. Leaves flutter and dance, buds swell, and shameless blossoms unfurl and offer themselves freely to the sky.

I can scarcely sleep at night; I am too restless with excitement. In the long green history of the world, there has never been a season such as this.

*If this is what love does to the world, how
could anyone plant a garden without it?*

IT IS STRANGE, keeping a secret from Father.

But it is wonderful, too, for with every passing day
that I resist telling Father what I know, Weed's secret
becomes my secret, and his truth is my truth as well.
I—only I!—know what magic he possesses, and the
mere act of knowing has transformed me from the
commonplace creature I was, to the singular, extraordinary creature I am now.

I am the girl who knows. The only person Weed
trusts.

I am the one he loves.

Father does suspect something, as Weed observed,
but even his wildest imaginings could not approach
the truth of Weed's gift. And that is not all that he suspects. This morning, as I stand in the kitchen washing
up, Father comes in and announces: "Jessamine, there
is a good chance I will have to return to London."

"When?"

159

"Soon. I may be gone a few days. I cannot say more about my business there, but as I may have to leave abruptly, I did not want you to worry."

"Oh, it is all right, Father," I say, perhaps a bit too quickly. "If I know that you are all right, I will manage."

"I expect you will." He clears his throat. "I do not want to leave you in a compromising position. I hope it is not imprudent for me to leave you and Weed here alone. You are both young, and—well, you seem to like each other a great deal."

I wring out my dish towel with undue concentration, as if it were the most interesting task imaginable.

"Do you love him?"

My blush provides all the answer Father needs.

"I see." He frowns. "I am surprised, yet I ought not be. If I have never imagined you growing up, falling in love, perhaps marrying and moving away—that is a failure of imagination on my part. Perhaps I never thought of it because I have lived so long as a bachelor, since your mother died . . . yet how could I forget what it was like? To be young, and in love."

He shakes off his reverie and resumes his usual authoritative tone. "Remember: This is my home, and Weed is our guest. In my absence you are his host. You may act toward him as such. As for love—be virtuous and use the judgment God gave you, Jessamine. You are still scarcely more than a—"

"Father, enough." I wheel from the sink. Soapy water drips from my hands onto the floor. "I will heed your words. But I am far from a child."

I expect he will be furious at my insolence, but I no longer care. Perhaps he senses this.

"My apologies, Jessamine," he says, inclining his head. "You are quite right. I may not think of you as full grown, but you are certainly not a child anymore."

He reaches toward me and lifts my hair away from my face. "In fact," he adds softly, "in this light, you look a great deal like your mother. May your virtue be rewarded with a longer, healthier life than hers."

In the afternoon I work in the herb bed, thinning out the weak seedlings and pinching back the rest, then laying down a fresh layer of rotted hay as mulch. Afterward Weed and I walk. He fills my head with tales from the ancient forests, tales so old that the trees themselves call them legends. It is as if a veil has been lifted from my eyes, and the world I have lived in all my sixteen years is revealed to be something else entirely, something so marvelous I could never have imagined it.

When we return to the cottage Father is gone: boots, coat, medical bag, and all. He must have received the summons to London he was expecting.

Father is entitled to his secrets, too, I tell myself, still giddy from the walk. *That is only fair, considering.*

Weed and I are alone. We have been alone together many times, of course, but now that Father has left, perhaps for days, our shared solitude is altered. It feels heightened, expectant, almost celebratory. *It is like playing house,* I think. *Imagine if this cottage were ours, just mine and Weed's—*

I prepare a fine dinner for the two of us, a spring stew of lamb, potatoes, and fresh greens. When the

162

food is ready I set the table and light candles. I find tea already made in the kitchen; I warm it and pour it into cups that I choose only after careful inspection.

Weed devours his food; I am pleased. We converse as we usually do during dinner, but after the meal is done our conversation lapses. It is different with just the two of us here. He feels it too, I can tell. It is delicious, this privacy: Which of us will be the first to mention it?

I sip my tea, and Weed sips his. All my senses begin to feel heightened. The candlelight twists and leaps. The linen napkin in my lap is pleasantly smooth to the touch. From outside I hear the anxious whir of crickets, and the soft *flep-flep-flep* of bats whizzing back and forth by the window.

I notice that the bucket I once used to soak the belladonna seeds is now set in a corner, partially filled with smooth pebbles. Father must be gathering them to rake into a path.

"I wonder why they call it belladonna?" I ask, breaking the silence. "'Lovely lady.' It is a strange name for a plant."

"They say it can be used to make a woman more beautiful."

I snort. "How? That is ridiculous."

"Perhaps, but that is what some believe."

I stir my cup, now nearly empty. "Have you ever seen it used? Does it work?"

"I have not seen it myself, but I am told that it has—a strong effect," Weed answers carefully.

"Then I must try it." I feel suddenly bold, silly, reckless.

"But you could not be made more beautiful," he says with a smile. "It would be impossible."

"I am sure the belladonna would disagree." I stand. "Come, Weed! You must show me how to do it." Laughing flirtatiously, I grab his hand. Where does this dizzy abandon come from? I scarcely feel the floor beneath my feet, as I half drag, half dance Weed to Father's study.

"There it is," I say, pointing to the high shelf. I could drag a chair over and stretch up for it, but there is no need—my mood has infected Weed, and he reaches the forbidden bottle easily.

"How does it work?" I ask as I twirl in front of the desk.

"A drop in each eye; that is all you need." Weed opens the jar and removes one of its precious dark pearls. It rolls lazily in his palm. "It will make your pupils widen, your eyes flash with fire—they say no man can resist its gaze."

"Do it," I plead, in a voice that sounds utterly unlike my own. "Make me beautiful, Weed. I wish to look at you with these flashing eyes you speak of."

With a gentle hand beneath my chin, he tilts my head back.

"Open your eyes wide, and look up," he instructs.

I do, and am forced to stare at the murals on Father's ceiling that are left over from the chapel days. I see Adam and Eve, alone in the garden, the tree of knowledge behind them, a serpent coiled around the overhanging branch from which dangles the delicious, forbidden fruit—

"Hold still, now—"

One—two—the drops burn like acid, and I cry out.

"It only stings for a moment," Weed soothes. "Now close your eyes—and when you are ready, open them."

You have both gone mad, some sane ghost of my former self scolds me—

Silence, I bid the ghost, and open my eyes. As soon as I do I know the drops have worked. I feel their powerful heat throughout my being. The belladonna drops have made me ravishing, sloe-eyed, worldly, irresistible—at least I imagine they have. The world is a blur. Each object melts into the next in a syrupy swirl of color.

"Weed, I cannot see," I complain.

"You do not need to," he replies. "You are to be admired."

"But I wish to know what *you* see when you look at me." I flail my arms about. "Where is the mirror?"

"Very well." Weed leads me to the glass. "Come, look. Admire yourself."

We stand together before the mirror. I can make out only shapes: a dab of yellow where my hair ought to be, floating above a long smudge that is more or less the color of the dress I dimly recall putting on this morning. The image swims before my eyes, turns liquid. Then, like parchment that gets too near a flame, the edges begin to go dark.

"Do you see?" Weed asks, from someplace far away. "Can you see how beautiful you are?"

I cannot. I cannot see anything now. The soft veil of darkness wraps around me. Weed's voice is my world, now. It caresses me like a breeze. Warms me like the sun.

I love him.

I turn and reach out until I find him. My blindness makes me bold. In this dim, private world, anything that might happen is merely a dream, a wisp, a fantasy. Nothing is forbidden.

I am blind, and I have never felt so free.

I cling to Weed's body, a landmark in the dark. Unseeing, I run my hands up his chest and twine them around his neck. I throw my head back, so that he may gaze into my charmed, useless eyes and be captivated by their spell.

"Lovely lady." His whisper coils around me like smoke. "*Belladonna.* My lovely, lovely Jessamine—"

I love you, Weed.

In the darkness I let myself melt, so he has no choice but to catch me and lift me, cradling my body against his. His mouth finds mine. After the first kiss I arch so his lips brush the tender skin of my throat instead.

Their warm, velvet touch sears me with pleasure. I would writhe in these flames forever, if it would keep his burning mouth pressed against me like this. I would stay eternally blind, if it meant my skin would always be this alive, every nerve on fire—

This is wrong, I think, but I have no wish to stop.

I love you, Weed; how I love you—

And are we not wed, bound by the secret only we two can share?

Together we sink to the floor. Weed whispers my name against my flesh. I feel his breath come faster. I want him to kiss me again, and say so. This fierce longing flies beyond the wildest notion of what is

168

proper, yet we are swept into each other by a relentless current—*the rush to fertility triumphs over all*—

I hear a distant thud, like a heavy door closing.

Stop, I whisper, but no sound comes out.

Weed freezes in my arms. He hears it too: the sound of a man's boots walking deliberately across ancient wooden floors. The footsteps get louder as they approach.

I hear Weed scramble to his feet. I reach down and try to smooth my skirt by touch alone. I can feel that one of my shoes is gone, but how will I ever find it without the use of my eyes?

A familiar creak; it is the door to Father's study opening.

There is a sharp intake of breath—an anguished cry—

"Father?" I stretch my arms forward, clawing at the dark fog that surrounds me. "Father, is that you?"

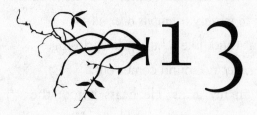

13

It is hours—days, weeks? I have no way of knowing—before the darkness begins to lift.

My head aches. So do my wrists. I am slumped in a chair, but I cannot tell where I am. I seem to be restrained, somehow.

"Forgive me," Father's voice murmurs. "You have been wild, running blindly, crashing into walls, tripping over furniture. I feared you would do yourself harm."

I blink, and blink again. The pitch-black night of my blindness has thinned to a pale gray fog that strips all color from the world. Through its mist I can begin to make out shapes.

There is the dining table, and the light slanting through tall, arched chapel windows. I am in the parlor, in Father's big chair that is usually pulled near the hearth. I try to move, but my arms are fixed tightly to my body.

Father looms before me.

"Now you have experienced, firsthand, the dubious charms of belladonna," he says flatly as he frees my bound limbs. "My countless warnings, ignored. And these are the consequences."

"I am so sorry, Father." I begin to weep.

"Why, Jessamine?" He leans close to me. "What if I had not come back when I did? A broken carriage wheel postponed the coach to London until morning—" His voice catches. "If not for this random circumstance that interrupted my journey, where would you be right now?"

Father straightens. Now I can see Weed, slumped at the far end of the table. His face is a wary mask. I open my mouth to speak his name, but I stop. The truth is I cannot fully remember all that happened between us. Memories, sensations, all are shrouded in fog—surely it was only a dream?

"I was young once, too," Father says. "I suppose it was inevitable that you would someday disobey me. I hope that this bout of painful blindness will teach you a lesson, Jessamine. One that could save your life— though I fear it is too late to salvage your virtue," he adds pointedly.

Weed shakes his head vehemently, and my heart swells with relief. I pray that he will deny that anything untoward happened, for even if I did lose my mind temporarily, I must believe that Weed would only protect me, and not take advantage—

"It was not the belladonna," is all he says.

"Is that so?" Father moves toward Weed so forcefully he knocks a chair to the ground. "Or is it possible that you do not know everything after all, Master Weed? It blinded her, though it seems she will recover, thank God. And, judging from what I witnessed when I walked into my study, it also seems to have removed some—*inhibitions.*" He turns away from me; his voice is suddenly cold. "I must confess: I did not know that belladonna could have that *particular* effect. I will have to make a notation about it in my book."

Father addresses Weed. "Can you two be trusted alone together? Or would it be wise to tie you to a chair as well, Master Weed?"

Weed clenches his jaw and turns away. Satisfied, Father leaves the parlor.

I am too mortified to speak. Weed cannot bring himself to look at me. The air between us is thick with shame.

It was not the belladonna. . . . I remember, now— yes, there was some strange abandon, a fever of recklessness that began to sweep over me, well before those cursed drops ever went in my eyes—before we had even entered the study. Weed and I were sitting at the table, sipping from those carefully chosen cups—

Put it this way, Luxton: The boy seems to know a thing or two about brewing a pot of tea. . . .

"No!" The cry rips itself from my throat. Weed is

173

at my side in an instant.

"Are you all right?" He kneels next to me. His hands hover around me, longing to comfort me but afraid to touch. His whole being seems to throb with concern and devotion.

I look at his face and will my raw, stinging pupils to focus, so that I may search for the truth in his eyes. Unfathomable moss green pools—surely that is love I see shining in their depths? Love, and worry, and nothing else but that?

Or have I been blind all along?

Remember, Jessamine—the tea was already made when you entered the kitchen—

No, no—

Weed would never do something like—like that.

"I'm convinced the brat put something in the tea." *Wasn't that what Pratt said?*

No!

Weed has trusted me with his darkest secret. And I trust him with my life.

But should I?

174

"Jessamine, my Jessamine," he whispers desperately, again and again. "Are you all right? Are you all right? Are you all right?"

29th May

My eyes are healing slowly, but they are not
yet well enough to sew. I wish they were, for I find
it too painful to work in the garden. Every green
living thing reminds me of Weed. How I envy
the plants! They can whisper to him all day, and
shelter him with their shade. But he and I are only
permitted to see each other in the evenings, in the
parlor, when Father is there.

We speak stiffly of the weather and bid each
other good night like strangers.

All day and all night I worry—will Father send Weed away?

It is like waiting for a coming storm, but there are no shutters I can bolt fast against the wind. When the gale comes, I fear it will blow my chance for happiness far, far away, never to be seen or heard from again.

Weed and I are so careful with each other now. We no longer take our walks together, for such luxuries of intimacy are no longer possible. The whole day long we live like brother and sister, chaste and respectful. But at night, I close my eyes and the dream that was no dream comes rushing back, its power undimmed. Then I toss in my bed, restless, exhausted yet unable to sleep.

Sometimes I think we ought to run away and marry. Sometimes I do not know what to think. Especially when I am alone in the kitchen, preparing tea. My hands shake as I pour the water. Now I can see that Tobias Pratt's accusations are the true poisons, for they have infected my thoughts with mistrust and suspicions that must be scrubbed away, again and again.

2nd June

Father asked me to prepare a special meal for this evening. I inquired whether we were having a

guest; he did not answer.

Is Tobias Pratt coming to take Weed away
again? It is all I can think of. Oh, I am sick at
heart.

Mutton chops, braised carrots, fresh bread, and a raisin
pudding for dessert. The work occupies me all afternoon. I am elbow-deep in soapsuds doing the washing
up when Father enters the kitchen and instructs me to
leave the pots and pans as they are, bathe, and change
into fresh clothes. "You might want to put on something pretty," he adds. As if I had a wardrobe of party
frocks to choose from! Whatever could he mean?

In spite of my dark mood I grow curious. Surely
Father would not make such a request if our guest were
the likes of Tobias Pratt? I wonder if the duke himself
might be paying a call, though for what purpose I cannot imagine. I have heard no hunters' guns today.

I follow Father's instruction as best I can. There is
a light muslin dress in my closet that was my mother's,
with a smocked bodice and delicate embroidery at the

hem and sleeve cuffs. The last time I tried it on, it dragged on the floor and was loose in the bodice, but now it seems to fit me well. I braid my damp hair and find a ribbon to tie around it. Even I scarcely recognize the womanly creature who gazes back at me from the mirror.

See? A memory croons in my ear. *Can you see how beautiful you are?*

The thought paints sudden color on my cheeks. Now I have no need of rouge; the heat of shame has provided the finishing touch to my toilette.

I enter the parlor, embarrassed to be seen in my mother's clothes. To my surprise Father himself has set the table, not with our everyday dishes, but with the fine gold-rimmed porcelain ones that were his and Mama's wedding china.

And—my heart skips a beat at the sight—Weed is there. Freshly bathed, dressed in a crisp white shirt, dark trousers, and Father's best jacket, with a scarlet silk lining. Even Father has changed shirts, and an ebony silk tie shines at his throat.

In this way the three of us, dressed as if it were Christmas Day, stand stupefied as mannequins. "Is it the duke who is coming?" I finally ask, unable to stay silent. "It must be; why else all this fuss, Father?"

Father laughs, deep and hearty. "Children," he says, extending his hands to both of us. "This feast is for you."

Weed and I look at each other, amazed. Father clasps both hands behind his back and explains. "A week ago today, I left this house with a mind to go to London. Returning only a few hours later, I discovered that in my absence there had been a transgression. We need not speak the details of it again." Father holds up a hand to secure our silence. "Please, let me finish. In the days since, I have reflected on this incident a great deal. I am sure you have as well. Now, let there be no mistake: My direct orders were disobeyed. For this there is no excuse; but you have repented, and I wish you to know that I forgive you."

"Father, you are too good—" I exclaim.

"Patience, Jessamine. A moment ago I called you

179

children, but I think we have seen—the transgression itself offered proof, as it were—that you are no longer children; far from it. I pride myself on my powers of observation, but sometimes a father is the last to see what is right before his eyes. The path ahead is clear: Jessamine, you must embrace the future that has already laid claim to you." He looks first at me, then at Weed. "It is my sincere wish, and my joyous expectation, that the two of you are betrothed at once."

Betrothed? To Weed?

Has my father gone mad? Or is he mocking us? This is my first thought. But no; he beams at the two of us, his hands outstretched in benediction. Kindness and forgiveness are written all over his face—he is like a stranger to me; I cannot remember ever seeing him like this.

Hot tears spill from my eyes. Tears of joy, tears of shock—tears of grief, too, for now I can never know if Weed would have asked me to be his wife without Father's prompting. Yet I must be grateful, for is this not what I wanted?

With this tumult of emotions whirling inside me, I look to my future husband for some clue as to the content of his heart. Weed's face remains inscrutable. After a moment he gives a small half bow.

"Thank you. I am glad you find me suitable."

Father nods. "I had hoped you would feel that way. As for Jessamine—I suppose I need not ask how she feels about the notion of marrying you; the answer is written on her face."

"Thank you, Father." My voice is scarcely more than a whisper. Suddenly shy, I wish nothing more than to run upstairs to the safety of my room. How I wish it were Weed himself who proposed! Then I could accept him with an open heart.

Father lays a hand on each of our shoulders. "Jessamine and Weed, my blessings upon you both. We are a family at last." He turns to me; tenderly he takes my face in his hands. "Jessamine, if your mother could only see what a lovely young woman you have grown to be, I know she would be pleased. How sad it is that she did not live to see you grown, or to see you wed . . ."

He drops his hands and turns away. "No, I refuse to be melancholy. Tonight is for happiness only, and Jessamine has prepared a wonderful celebration dinner for us. But first, a toast."

Father fairly skips around the parlor. "Most proud fathers would call for champagne to toast an engagement. But I have none on hand, nor any wine either. Only a rather common whiskey, and my store of absinthe. Ah, wait!"

He turns and reaches up to the small cabinet that hangs above the heavy wooden server. "This too is absinthe"—he cradles the bottle in two hands—"but it is a very special vintage, worthy of the occasion. Jessamine, fetch a pitcher of cold water, please."

I obey, and return to find Father explaining to Weed: "The duke gave this bottle to me as a gift after I cured his clerk of works of a crippling gout. It had been presented to him by King Louis of France, shortly before the revolution."

As he speaks, Father gathers three glasses from the server, a corkscrew, and an ornate slotted silver spoon. "Ironic, isn't it? King Louis lost his head to the guillotine, but his prize liquor is still firmly in possession of its cork. I have been waiting for a special occasion to open it. How thrilling that the right moment is finally here."

There is a sharp sound as Father withdraws the cork. He pours a small amount of absinthe in each of the three short, flared glasses, then places a cube of sugar in the slotted spoon and sets the spoon atop a glass. Slowly he drizzles cold water into the spoon, letting it drip through the sugar. As the water hits the syrupy absinthe, it whirls into ribbons, a tiny maelstrom of green.

Father hands the finished drink to Weed and makes another for himself. Then he repeats the process to prepare mine. "For Jessamine, an extra cube of sugar, I think," he says with a smile. "The taste will be too strong otherwise."

He hands the glass to me. I am unaccustomed to drink, but the scent is sweet licorice, not unpleasant at all. And the otherworldly green of the drink reminds me of Weed's eyes; I wonder if he will notice the similarity?

"What a rich, vibrant hue. It is a garden in miniature, is it not?" Father sniffs his drink appreciatively. "Now, for our toast: To my lovely daughter, Jessamine. And to my new son, Weed." He gazes warmly at us both. "To your health!"

"Thank you for all we are about to receive," says Weed, raising his glass to his lips.

I do the same. The licorice perfume, the burn of alcohol, the sweetness of the sugar give way to a bitter, metallic taste that coats my tongue. The complex flavor makes me want to take another sip, and then another.

"Delicious, isn't it?" Father remarks. "Notice how the mixture turns cloudy after a moment. Truly, it is a most unusual and botanical beverage; you can see why I prefer it to all others. . . ."

Fascinated, I stare into the absinthe. Sparkling multicolor gems float and bob on the surface of the creamy green sea, like survivors of a shipwreck. A kaleidoscope of light dances within the confines of my glass.

My eyes are still behaving strangely, I think.

"Now I hope neither of you will make a habit of taking strong drink," Father says jovially. "But on a special occasion—such as an engagement!—a proper toast is certainly called for."

An engagement . . . Dear Weed—he will be my husband, and with Father's blessing! It does feel like a dream, but I could never dream Father in such a celebratory mood.

Suddenly I long for Weed to know the joy I feel, but I cannot speak words of love in front of Father. Yet surely someone who can hear the whispered secrets of a dandelion can easily discern my all-too-human heart's promises of devotion, and see the adoration shining in my eyes?

I search Weed's face, seeking some answering vow of love in the arrangement of his features. If only we were alone, and could speak freely—the occasion overwhelms me, and I begin to feel unsteady—

"What do you think of the absinthe, Jessamine?" Father asks. "I hope it is not too potent for you. Perhaps it is a trick of the light, but it looks as though you are turning nearly the same green color yourself."

"I think—I think I feel sick," I say, and then I do not know what comes next, for I faint to the floor so quickly that not even Weed can catch me.

14

"Jessamine? Jessamine?"

Weed stands over me, swaying back and forth. That is not right—Weed is still; it is the room that sways. I clutch at the blankets—*there are blankets upon me, I am likely in my own bedchamber, then*—and try to sit up. Instead I nearly slip sideways off the bed.

"Not yet, dear Jessamine," Weed says tenderly. "Lie still."

I obey, for I can do nothing else. "What happened?"

"You drank a toast, and then took a sip, and then a

swallow, and finished the rest of the glass, every drop, before we could prevent you."

My eyes flutter closed; I am too weary to keep them open. "I am not fit to drink real liquor, it seems."

He squeezes my hand. "Rainwater is best."

I try to smile; it makes my head throb. "Do you really want me to be your wife?" I ask.

"Of course," he says, and kisses my palm.

"No toasts at the wedding, though," I murmur, drifting off again.

"Thank you for all that she is about to receive. Come, you must eat something."

I am sitting up, pillows stuffed behind my back. It appears that Weed has been feeding me soup, for now he is trying to nudge my lips open with the spoon. I do not even remember him coming in.

I breathe in the fragrant, herb-scented steam. I can feel the hunger and thirst that rack my body, but it is as if the sensations belong to someone else; I have no wish to swallow anything. I turn my head away and slump back into the pillows.

"You can do better than that," Weed insists. "You must. Remember how you persuaded me to eat?"

"I have no taste for it yet. I will eat when I am feeling better." I note the frown on his face. "Why do you seem so worried? Surely I am not the first person in the world to be made ill by drink. It will pass—*mmph*."

He sneaks one spoonful of broth into my mouth as I finish speaking. "Many times I saw how the friar made himself sick with too much ale. He would sleep like a dead man, and the next day wake in the foulest of moods. His head would hurt for a while; he would rage and complain. By nightfall he would recover and be ready to start the process all over again."

"Would you prefer me to be in a foul mood, then?"

"You can be, if you like." He places his cool hand on my forehead and brushes back my hair. The concern in his eyes cannot be hidden.

"Weed." I struggle to sit up again. "How long have I been in bed?"

His face pales, but his voice remains nonchalant. "Not long. Two or three days."

Three days? How can that be? I try to rise again, and the room spins so fast I fall back to the bed in an instant.

"This is not from the drink, then?"

He shakes his head.

"Am I ill?"

"I think so."

"Ill from what?"

He pauses. "I do not know."

A tight knot of fear forms in my chest. "Where is Father?"

"He went to London, early yesterday morning. He did not know how ill you were when he left. You were still sleeping, then, though restless and hard to wake." Gently he lays a hand on my forehead. "He too thought you were sickened by the drink."

"It was worth it to mark our engagement." I close my eyes, but they fly open again as a sudden thought pierces my feverish brain. I reach for Weed's hand.

"Weed, do you think the plants might offer a cure for my sickness?"

"I have already asked," Weed says anxiously. "I have walked the gardens, the fields, the forest. They say your condition is not of their making, and thus cannot be of their curing."

"'Not of their making'; what does that mean?"

"I am not sure." His voice catches. "It troubles me, Jessamine. They have always been eager, even proud, to offer their cures, even before I ask for them. Now they seem—frightened."

My eyes close of their own will. "Whatever is wrong, Father will cure me. I know he will," I mumble drowsily.

"I know he will try," I hear Weed say as I sink back into sleep.

"How much food has she taken?"

"Very little. I have got a few spoonfuls of the broth you prepared past her lips every quarter of an hour."

191

"Have you given her anything else? Any medicines, ointments, remedies?"

"No, sir."

My hand flies up, lifted by some force outside me, a puppet arm on a string.

"The pulse is weak and fast. Her color is sallow; the skin is cool. Jessamine? Can you speak?"

The words come out as an unintelligible moan, which is just as well, for I am prattling gibberish: *But Father, why can I not enter the 'pothecary garden? I am not a child anymore. . . .*

My hand sinks back to the bed. The voices wash over me, lapping each other like waves—

"She is delirious with fever."

"What can be wrong with her? The illness came upon her so quickly, with no warning."

The sharp snap of the latch on Father's medical bag. Bottles clinking against bottles.

"Believe it or not, there is a condition known as lovesickness."

"Mr. Luxton, do not joke—"

"I am completely serious. For a young woman like Jessamine, innocent, sheltered, with a sensitive and passionate temperament—it is possible that this has all been too much for her. The excitement has worn out her nerves; her body and mind are overwhelmed and seek respite in the only way they can: through a withdrawal into illness."

"Are you suggesting that I leave her?" Weed's voice is strangled. "For I will not—I cannot—"

"*Noooooo.*" An animal howl of protest escapes my lips.

Silence.

"Good." Father says after a moment. "Though she is unconscious, it seems she can hear us; that is a positive sign. No, Weed, I would not instruct you to be anywhere but by her side. At this point your departure would only make matters worse. Rest assured, I do not think lovesickness is the sole explanation for her condition. Rather, the excitement created by your engagement may have weakened her constitution temporarily, and thus made her susceptible to some disease or infection."

I thrash in the bed. Why do they talk about me so, as if I am not here? Do they think I am dead? With enormous effort I open my eyes. The light plunges into them like hot knives, but before I close them again I see Weed and Father standing shoulder to shoulder at the foot of the bed, shielding themselves from me. Their voices sink to hushed whispers; I can scarcely make out the words.

"Here; I have prepared a tincture of catnip and hyssop for the fever; cinnamon to fight any infection, boiled mallow roots as a tonic, cloves to purify the blood, hawthorn to strengthen her heart—do you agree?"

After a moment, a low, hoarse reply: "It will not do any harm. I am without any further knowledge in this matter. Sir, please do as you think best."

A pause.

"Very well. Give her one spoonful every ten minutes. She may not care for the taste, but it cannot be helped."

The door closes. Father has left the room, I can

sense it. Weed's weight settles on the edge of the bed. Reflexively I curl toward him, like a sunflower bending toward the sun.

"Take this," he pleads. "It is medicine, to cure you. Just one spoonful, my dear one."

I obey. It is thick and tastes of sour milk, kerosene, sulfur, mold—the vile, oily mixture gurgles down my throat. I am too weak to gag.

"Is it awful?"

I shake my head no, and force my cracked lips into an imperceptible smile.

"Let it make you better," Weed urges.

"I will." I half open my eyes, ignoring the stabbing pain that results. "See? I am stronger already."

He looks at me as if I am dying.

I love you, I tell him without words.

"Jessamine," he says sadly. "Oh, my poor Jessamine. What have I done to you?"

Time passes, unmeasured. My illness persists. The fever comes and goes; I can tell from the dull pressure inside my skull as it rises, and the way I shiver and shake with chills when it recedes. When the fever is at its worst, my mind overflows with strange, blurred images.

Sometimes I think I can see figures out of the corners of my eyes. When I turn my head to look, they vanish. Only the sounds remain: the whir of beating wings, a soft creak of tree branches in the wind, a low hum that rises and falls like the swell of murmuring voices.

There are other voices, too:

The medicine is not working.

Obviously it is not! If you have a better suggestion I would appreciate hearing it.

I am sorry. I wish I could be of some help, but I have none to offer.

That is hardly sufficient.

Father is in a rage; I listen to him bellow:

"A stranger—an idiot!—strikes his foot with an ax, and you overflow with remedies. But now, nothing. She is to be your wife! Why now, when her life is in the balance, do you have only apologies? Is there nothing that can shake that mysterious medical wisdom from your head?"

A pause.

"Perhaps, Weed—if you went into the apothecary garden—"

"Why do you say that?"

"The plants in there are powerful. If you examine them closely, you may be able to discover a means to help her."

What? But Weed promised me he would not go into the poison garden again! He cannot, it is too dangerous for him, I will not permit it—

"Perhaps you are right—but I am afraid—let us talk elsewhere, please."

They leave me.

I am alone, again.

If Weed ever returns, I think, I will ask him to dress me in Mama's wedding dress. I want him to see me in it, once before I die.

The sky has turned yellow as a dandelion.

The clouds swirl like vicious whirlpools in the sky,

as if they would devour all the earth below. When I dare look out the window I feel myself being lifted up, drawn into its leering maw.

I squeeze my eyes shut and wail. I clutch the blankets and cling tightly to the bed. My body pulls upward, eager for the end. It wants to float away and disappear into that roiling, ravenous mouth.

I do not know how much longer I can hold on.

Weed comes to see me and spoons horrors into my mouth. I try to tell him about the sky. I want to ask him to draw the curtains shut, or tie me fast to the mattress so I cannot be stolen by that gaping hole in the heavens. But no words emerge from my lips. No sound from my throat but a tiny, frightened mewing.

This is the only voice I have left—the sound of a newborn kitten abandoned by its mother, sightless, helpless, knowing nothing of life but thirst and cold, and a faint animal instinct rising from the gut, say-ing *this is not how it was supposed to be*—to make the long journey from whatever comes before birth, to be brought forth with such effort and wailing, only to be snuffed out again so quickly—

Poor kitten, I think. If mama cat does not come back soon, it will be too weak to cry for help. The end will come quickly then.

At least, when it comes, the black night of death will not frighten a creature still blind from being born. That is some comfort, is it not?

No. No. No. I am no dying kitten. I am a sick girl, sick with something strange and rare. Something Weed cannot help me with. Something the healing plants of the earth stubbornly refuse to name.

Something that Father will soon figure out how to cure.

But I thought your father knew how to cure everything?

Everything but what ails me, I suppose—

Wait.

Who are you?

15

7th June

WRITTEN BY THE YOUTH KNOWN AS WEED

*A strange storm broods in the northeastern sky.
The air is heavy and smells of the sea. The earth
stinks of sickness and decay.*

Hour by cursèd hour, Jessamine is getting worse.

JESSAMINE IS TOO ILL to continue writing the garden diary. Mr. Luxton has asked me to keep it in her stead. I will try to do so, though my handwriting is poor. I wish she were writing here instead of me.

She is so ill! It fills me with anger, though I cannot say at whom I am angry, and grief, though she is not dead. I find myself amazed at the passion that has taken root inside me. I have never had a strong affection for any human creature before, but now, all at once, there is one whom I am certain I could not bear to lose.

She rolls in her bed, feverish, moaning, and calling out strange words. Her hands grab at the sheets until her nails cut into her palms. The skin on her knuckles cracks and bleeds.

Sometimes she stares out the window and cries out, "*No, no, no,*" but if I draw the shutters, the darkness frightens her more. She makes raw sounds, sharp like a crow. I do not know if she can tell I am there. I spoon water and medicine to her lips. I sit. I watch. My tears fall like rain.

Today I will enter the poison garden, as Jessamine's father has asked me to, in the hopes of finding a cure.

If only he knew the dark mission he sends me on!

But he is right—the plants in his locked garden possess great power. If there is a cure for her, it may well lie within those walls.

His request shocked me. Has Mr. Luxton guessed my "gift"? No, for it would take a madman to suspect the truth, and Luxton is the opposite of mad. For him there are no visions, no miracles, no curses, no witch-craft. There are only discoveries. Things unknown that can be made known. At least he will not suspect me of some dark magic, as Tobias Pratt did.

I do not know what will become of me, once I enter that place. I only know that Jessamine is failing, and the healing plants cannot, or will not, help me. I have begged them, on my knees in the dirt. They offer nothing! The plants whisper mysterious warnings to me. They keen with grief and then fall silent. Their refusal leaves me no choice.

They too are afraid of the poison garden. Something has happened inside those tall gates, where so many deadly herbs have been gathered in one spot.

Some new, dangerous power has gathered itself and been loosed upon the world. It is strange to say, but I can only think it is something unnatural.

Earlier, even before dawn, I sat by the bed and told Jessamine what I intended to do. I asked her permission, for I know she did not wish me to go into that horrible place again. I asked her forgiveness for breaking my promise, but I do not think she heard me.

It is time. I dread the poison garden. I dread what might happen to me inside those tall gates. The plants in there are dangerous. They are far cleverer than I am; I know that. They will try to trick me, perhaps destroy me. But deep in my soul, I believe they will know what is wrong with her.

I would give my life to save Jessamine. I may have to.

Look. Look how beautiful I am.

I am in Mama's wedding dress. Now it is made of cream-colored rose petals that caress me as I walk. Every step I take is perfumed.

When I am tired of taking steps, I float. I can float anywhere, go anywhere, be anywhere. I am borne on the wind like a tuft of dandelion, a feather, a speck.

A ghost.

I wonder if I am dead?

Before, when I was well and fully alive, I used to long to know what might be happening inside the castle at Alnwick, or in a big, faraway city like London, or in the vast Canadian wilderness across the sea, or even in that awful war in France. My whole life, Hulne Park has been my world and prison. I thought it would be so wonderful to see something else, though I had no real hope of doing so.

Now I can travel to all those places, and more. I am untethered! Time, distance, even Father's forbidding gaze—none of these pose any obstacle to me anymore.

So where shall I go? If I were to gain entry to the castle I know I would not spend all my time in the library, as Father does. There would be so much else to see! The grand staterooms and the dining hall, the scullery and the parapets, the armory full of weapons that were used to push back the Scots—

Curious. It feels as if there is still someone else here, hovering, close by. I do not know who he is, but it is nice not to be alone.

If he wishes to become friends, perhaps we will fly together.

Mr. Luxton brings me to the gate of the poison garden and unlocks it. Already I hear the cruel voices calling to me, luring me to quicksand.

"Be careful, Weed." He pockets the ring of keys. "I would not have you fall ill as well."

I shrug. "It does not matter. I have no choice but to go in."

"I wish you would let me accompany you." Agitated, he stands between me and the gate. "There are many specimens in there, rare and deadly—you ought not be left alone with them."

"No." My voice is rough with impatience. "I must go alone, or not at all. I cannot explain."

"As you wish." He turns and lets the chain slip free of the lock. The padlock falls to the ground, but his hand lingers on the latch. "Once Jessamine is saved, perhaps you will be willing to tell me why."

"Once Jessamine is saved," I repeat dumbly. My heart pounds. The coven of sirens within calls my name, soft and sickly sweet—

Weed . . . Weed . . .

"Remember," he warns. "Do not touch anything. If you feel ill, call for me at once. I will wait here for you at the entrance—"

Weed . . .

"I must go in now," I say. "Step aside; I beg you."

Luxton still bars my way. "You do love her, don't you, Weed? My daughter's life is in your hands! I must know your true heart."

"Of course I love her." My anger rises; I have no time to stand here talking. My Jessamine is dying and the beings that could save her summon me. I cannot keep them waiting any longer.

"Good luck to you, then." Looking grim, Luxton pushes open the gate.

Hello? There you are—I knew there was someone here. Why are you hiding?

I have come to welcome you, but I did not wish to alarm you. I thought you might find it strange if I appeared too suddenly.

Everything is strange to me. I was well; then I became sick, and now I am—I do not know what I am. I can fly, though.

It is lovely to have wings. Mine are large and black, like a raven's. Yours are gossamer; they catch the light quite beautifully.

We have wings? How wonderful! But who are you? And what is this misty realm? Is it heaven, or hell? Are we alive or dead?

So many questions! I will answer as best I can: I am alive, though not quite in the way you are used to. You are neither alive nor dead, but something in between. This misty realm is my home. Heaven and hell have no meaning to me; you will have to decide for yourself what place this more nearly resembles.

You still did not say who you are.

Among my own kind I am a prince.

A prince! I am embarrassed now; I have never met anyone of title but the Duke of Northumberland, and I was much too awkward and shy to speak to him directly.

Nonsense; you are the embodiment of grace and charm, and as full of beauty as a rosebud at dawn.

That is a pretty compliment, thank you. Forgive my ignorance: What realm do you have dominion over, Your Majesty?

You have visited there yourself, Jessamine, though you did not stay long. Do you not recognize me?

I am sorry, I do not. But I am not myself at the moment. I feel as if I have forgotten many things, important things—and how did you know my name?

There is no need to apologize. We have all the time in the world to get to know each other. I am Oleander, the Prince of Poisons.

The gate to the poison garden closes behind me with a loud clang, as final as death.

The last time I set foot here, I clenched my mind

208

against the voices. On that day Jessamine walked next to me and served as my anchor, my guide, my light.

Now I do more than surrender—willfully I lose myself in the dark realm of the Poisons. I let the mist swirl around me until all trace of human existence is gone. It feels like I am falling, and I do not know how or if I will ever find my way back.

I look around at the poison garden, so familiar, yet so changed. Everything I see appears as if through a fine silver curtain. The plants are sharp and bare as skeletons.

"He has come!" a child's voice trills. "We called him and called him, and now he is here."

I remember the cacophony of voices from my earlier visit here, and wonder if I have heard that piping squeal before. I sink to one knee so I may better address its source. "Who are you?" I ask the tall stalks with their delicate blue flowers.

"I am Larkspur, Master Weed. I have tried to speak to you many times, but you have been terribly rude. Always ignoring me. I know it is because I am poisonous.

If I were dull and harmless and empty-headed as a daisy you would like me better, probably. I find it very unfair! For I cannot help being what I am."

"Just as you cannot help being what you are, Master Weed." The voice booms like thunder.

I rise and seek the source of this new presence, but the voice addresses the other plant. "Don't mope, Larkspur. It's no day for throwing tantrums. We have a visitor, after all, and when was the last time that happened? Four years past? Or was it forty?"

"Are you thinking of the old healer woman, Dumbcane?" It is a third voice, smooth and melodious, and comes from a woody vine with large flat leaves and tiny, grapelike fruits. "I remember her. She came here once, full of clever questions, and we never saw her again."

The broad-leaved plant called Dumbcane laughs and replies, "That's because they burned her at the stake, Moonseed."

"Be careful what you ask to know, Master Weed, for knowledge can be dangerous. So sayeth Moonseed."

"True—but the people who are afraid of knowl-edge are more dangerous still." The seductive voice comes from close behind me. Startled, I turn.

"I am Snakeweed," the delicate, lacy shrub croons. "Not every poison is bitter, Master Weed. Remember that."

"I bet he already knows," chirps Larkspur. "I bet he knows plenty about poison—"

"Quiet, sprout," Dumbcane says. "Now make your request, Master Weed. You must have a reason for coming here. Everyone does."

"Some are so unhappy they wish to die," Moonseed says dreamily.

"Others are so unhappy they wish to kill." Snakeweed's voice holds a sneer.

"And some are so unhappy they wish to forget who they are, and what the source of their misery is, and even who it was they once wished to kill." Larkspur laughs in delight.

"I come seeking a cure," I begin. "Not for myself. For a young lady. Jessamine Luxton is her name. She

211

lies in her sickbed, feverish and weak. I do not know what ails her. Will you help me?"

"And what about your usual friends? The chamomile? The peppermint? The feverfew? I suppose they are of no use to you today." Snakeweed's yellow flowers tremble with fury. "You prefer them to us—until you need something only we can give. Then you crawl to us, like ivy."

"Poison ivy, you mean!" Larkspur's giggle pierces my ears.

"What you say may be true," I confess. "But I must find a cure for her, and I do not care where it comes from."

"Your kind do not come to us for cures," Snakeweed snarls. "You come seeking power over life and death, for life and death are what we have to offer."

"And our assistance comes at a price," Moonseed adds.

"I offer you everything I have." Knowing I have nothing, I add, "And anything you ask for, I will give."

Dumbcane laughs, deep and mocking. "No need to be dramatic. All we ask is that you perform a few simple tasks. Merely to prove your resolve."

"Even if what you bid me do is impossible, I will find a way," I declare.

"How righteous he sounds, and how brave!" Larkspur's giggle rises to nearly a shriek. "Lucky for you, the first task is an easy task. The hardest part is doing nothing."

"Tear a leaf from me, Master Weed," Moonseed instructs, "and I will guide you."

"With pleasure," I say, and rip the leaf with as much brutality as I can.

You must not eat those, Prince Oleander. They are dangerous.

Do you mean these delicious berries, plump and black as ebony pearls? You are mistaken, Jessamine. Look, I eat them all day as if they were sweets. Would you like to try one?

Father always warned me—

Ten will kill a live person. They can do no harm to a dead one.

213

And what of a person who is someplace in between?

That is hard to say. Perhaps they will make you well. Perhaps they will make you worse. There is only one way to find out. Here.

They look so tempting, it is hard to resist.

No need to resist, allow me—

But—oh! So sweet! I thought it would be tart.

I am glad you like them, lovely. Careful, you would not want to drip the juice on that exquisite garment. Why, you look as if you are dressed to be married, Jessamine! Surely you are too young to do something so permanent?

I am recently betrothed to a boy named Weed.

How unfortunate. The name, I mean. Straggling, intrusive Weed: He loves you, I suppose? And you love him, too?

I do, but I am also disappointed in Weed right now, for he made me a solemn promise, and I fear he is breaking it even as we speak.

What promise was that?

That he would never go into Father's locked apothe-

214

cary garden again. It is an awful place, do you know it?

I know it very well, in fact. My colleagues are there, my companions. My subjects, if you will.

I am sorry! I did not mean to offend.

Only a fool takes offense at the truth, Jessamine. They are awful, of that there is no question. But they are also very charming. Purveyors of unspeakable suffering and indescribable delights. Performers of murders and miracles! You might grow to like them, if you got to know them as I do. But why has your beloved Crabgrass ventured into this garden of horrors, I wonder?

He thinks he can cure me, if the plants there will tell him how.

Clever Weed! He is right.

Will they tell him?

My subjects will do as I wish, of course.

And what will you bid them do?

Hmm. I am not sure yet, actually.

What—would you let me die? Oleander, you are frightening me! Are you killing me? Am I already dead?

Hush now. Don't be afraid, my lovely. We are friends.

Here, have another belladonna berry. It will soothe your nerves.

No, please, I do not want to—

But you must. And they truly are delicious, have another, good girl. Poor thing, look at you, you are all atremble now—see how your petals flutter in the wind? It suits you. I would always have you thus, trembling like this, with that enchanting, irresistible gaze . . . how fragile and lovely you are, my lovely, lovely lady . . .

16

MOONSEED GUIDES ME through cascading fountains of silver mist. When my vision clears, I see we have arrived at a familiar sheep meadow, not far from Hulne Abbey.

"You can leave the poison garden," I say, the torn leaf clutched in my hand.

"Of course." That smooth voice talks quietly in my ear, though fainter than before. "We are not like other plants, Weed. You already knew that. Otherwise you would not have come to us for help—now look around; do you know where we are?"

"Yes." *I have lain in this grass with Jessamine,* I think. *Whatever happens to me now, it is for her sake.* The thought gives me strength.

I listen for the voices of the meadow grass, to see if they will offer me comfort. An anxious hum is all I hear. The plants fear for me, but fear more for themselves. What are they afraid of?

"Do you see what is happening there, in that open field?"

I look. A ewe has wandered away from the flock. She secludes herself near a small group of trees. Her belly is swollen, heavy with pregnancy. She paws the ground, lies down briefly, and then climbs to her feet again, restless with discomfort. Her bleat is low and urgent.

"That ewe is about to give birth," I say. "Is that what you want me to watch?"

"Yes. But we are not the only ones here. Look up."

I look. High in the branches of a hackberry tree, a raven perches. Its black eyes fix on the ewe, staring hungrily.

218

The anxious hum of the meadow grass rises into a cry of anguish. Already I fear what is going to happen.

"There is no prey for a raven here," I say, hoping it is true.

"Not yet. But there will be." The raven's cold, merciless eye stays fixed on the laboring ewe. "The raven will devour the lamb as it is being born," Moonseed says unemotionally. "The ewe will be unable to flee or defend herself, or her babe."

I think of the journey Jessamine and I took to the castle at Alnwick, and the grief of the mother we saw mourning her child. Sickened, I reach to the ground for a stone to hurl at the bloodthirsty bird. Moonseed interrupts: "Remember: The first task is to do nothing."

The ewe groans and sinks to the ground. She rolls onto her side. It is time.

Kraaaaaaaaaaaaaaaaaaaaah! The raven beats its wings and screams in excitement.

"But she is helpless," I protest. "Hear her cries;

219

the lamb is coming—"

"The task is to watch, and do nothing."

"But why?"

"If you seek the power to avert death, you must also be able to do nothing in the face of death. For no healer can be everywhere, and not every death can be—or should be—prevented. Look, it begins: The birth, and the raven awaits. Look, Weed, look. . . ."

It seems I am still alive—or dead—or in between.

I think Oleander is gone. He has fallen silent, at least. But I am not alone. I am flying again, borne on the wings of a great black bird. Its feathers are odd, though: long, dark, and narrow, like leathery, pointed leaves.

I look down as we fly—below us is Hulne Park. I see the cottage, the courtyard, the footpath, the sheep meadows, the forest. They look miniature, like child's toys. How marvelous to see everything that is familiar to me from such a strange, impossible vantage.

We arc and rise over the sheep meadows. Now I can see a person also, with a familiar shape and posture, wearing Father's old coat. It is Weed.

Weed!

I call, but he does not look up. Can he even see me, I wonder? He stands at the edge of a field, facing a copse of hackberry trees. There is a sheep, a ewe, alone in the shade of the branches. She lies on the ground, struggling to rise, but cannot. I wonder if she is injured?

As if reading my mind, my black-feathered steed flies closer, dipping down to get a better view. No, I can see everything now: She is lambing, and not easily, judging from her cries. The babe dangles from its mother, half born, still in the glistening wet sac. Something else is there too, something that also glistens, black and bloodred—

No!

Oh, if I were there, I would fight the wicked bird! I would kill it myself!

Weed! Can you hear me?

Why do you not save the lamb?

In terrible silence I trudge through the silver mist. Moonseed's voice guides me, and soon I am back in the poison garden. Moonseed, Dumbcane, Snakeweed, and Larkspur quiver expectantly in the garden beds.

I do not wait to be addressed, for I am sick at heart at what I have been forced to watch, and wish this to be over with quickly. "I have completed the task you sent me to do," I say flatly, throwing Moonseed's torn leaf on the ground.

"Poor Weed," Snakeweed purrs. "You must feel so guilty."

"I did not kill the lamb. The raven did."

"But you did nothing to help."

"No."

"You watched without flinching. You did not turn away, and you did not intervene." Dumbcane guffaws. "So there is no difference between you and the raven—except the raven got to eat, ha ha!"

"Truly, you are cold and heartless, just as your beloved Jessamine said!" Larkspur sings out. "A freak with no pity for any life that is not green!"

"I did as you instructed." I struggle to contain my anger. "Now give me a cure for Jessamine."

"You have not earned a cure. Not yet." A small bundle wrapped in leaves and tied with braided grass rolls through the mist toward my feet. I loosen the tie and look within: It is a mixture of leaves, twigs, seed-pods, and roots. Some are familiar to me; some are not. "Brew this into a tea," Dumbcane instructs. "It will ease her suffering for a while."

"Only a short while, though," Larkspur says gaily.

"It will keep her alive," Dumbcane adds, "long enough for you to perform your second task."

Oleander? Is that you?

I have been here all along, lovely. We have been flying together, you and I.

These are your wings, then, which bear me aloft?

Of course. Do you think I would entrust you to any-one else? Tell me: What do you think of your beloved Crabgrass now? Surely you could not marry a man so cruel and heartless, so lacking in feeling as he is? Why, he did nothing but watch as that evil bird feasted on the poor—

223

Please, do not say it.

But he did nothing. You admit that.

He must—he must have had his reasons.

He is shockingly ignorant, you know. He only knows what his leafy little friends tell him. And it is so easy to mistake one plant for another. Monkshood root for horseradish. Hemlock for carrots. Tragic errors, but they happen. Frankly, I am surprised he has lasted this long. If you married him, you would doubtless be a widow within a fortnight.

Are you threatening to trick him into eating poison if I marry him?

I merely state a hypothetical probability. Although . . . if I could be absolutely certain that this absurd engagement were called off, I would be rather more inclined to give Mr. Lamb Killer the cure for your condition. The only thing worse for Weed than you dying would be if you survived, only to reject him. His suffering would be exquisite!

Why do you wish him to suffer?

Call it professional interest. You see, Jessamine, love

is a kind of poison; one of my favorite kinds, in fact. It infects the blood; it takes over the mind; it seizes dominion over the body. It amuses me to think of him pining for you. Aching for what he cannot have. The loneliness in his soul festering like a wound. There is nothing I could do to him that is worse than what you have already done, my lovely. And I assure you, in his case there will be no cure.

And what of my suffering? My loneliness?

Immaterial. You will have me.

But I do not want you!

My sweet, sheltered flower, how could you possibly know what you want? If you stay with me, I will keep you wrapped in the pleasantest dreams. You will remember nothing that pains you. You will exist in a state of perpetual delight. I will adore you, Jessamine. I will shield you. I will intoxicate you.

And if I resist, what then? Will you punish me?

You will not be able to resist. That is the beauty of it.

Yes, I will—

Shhhh. Soon you will know what I mean. Come, it is

time to fly. They are trying to take you back from me now, and they will—but only for a brief, little while—

We soar through a storm, my black-winged tormentor and I. I cannot control his flight, I can only hang on his strange, waxy feathers with all my strength and pray that I do not fall. He ascends steeply through the churning gray clouds, faster and faster, as if pursued by some invisible, demonic predator.

Then, with no warning, he plummets. The air is so dense with fog I cannot even see the ground racing up to meet us. I open my mouth to scream, but a cold wind blows my cries inward. My mouth fills with an icy, foul-tasting rain.

After a moment I hear voices.

"Henbane. Mandrake root. What else was in the tea?"

"Mallow and feverfew."

The scratch of a pen. "Fascinating. This information is priceless, priceless."

The cold, hard edge of a metal spoon presses against my lip.

Now I lie in darkness—true, simple darkness, the kind that comes from having one's eyes shut against the light. The firmness beneath me is not the feathered bed of a raven's back, but the length and breadth of my own straw-stuffed mattress.

The word emerges from my lips with a will of its own. "Weed—"

"Look! She wakes."

I open my eyes. The first thing I see is Weed's face. I seize his arm and dig my fingers into his flesh.

"Do not go back inside that garden," I beg. "Promise me, Weed. You must not go near it!"

"Jessamine—my darling—you are alive—"

"There is evil there, the Poisons will destroy us all—swear to me, Weed! I will not release you until you swear it!" I clutch him harder. My nails pierce his skin like talons until the blood flows. He cries out in pain, and the spoon that was in his hand clatters to the ground.

"Yes, of course I promise—I swear."

I let go of him. He cradles his wounded arm and

stares at me as if I have gone mad.

"Better to let me die like the lamb—than to go back there," I manage to say, before collapsing back on the bed.

30th June

Jessamine is awake. She knows me, and has been
able to speak a few words. My heart fills with hope,
yet I must remember what the Poisons told me:
This is no cure, merely a respite. She could slip
away from us again at any time.

Better to let me die like the lamb. That is what she said.

How did she know about the lamb? She, who lay silent and icy lipped on the bed the whole time I endured that wretched task? While her body fails, what strange journeys does she take in the fevered prison of her mind?

If she were a healing herb or even a blade of grass,

I would hear her very thoughts. But she is flesh—frail and all too mortal. A blank to me.

I wish I could heed her warning about the poison garden. I wish I knew what she fears, and why. But the Poisons say there are two more tasks for me to perform before I have earned her cure, and I cannot flinch now.

Even Mr. Luxton agrees. He was seized with joy when he saw the bundled remedy the Poisons provided. Even as I boiled the water to brew the mixture into a tea for Jessamine, he carefully copied into his book a faithful rendering of every leaf, twig, and seed in the mixture the Poisons had given me.

"If we are to save Jessamine, we must learn everything we can," he said, blotting the pages. "You must keep up your courage, and go back, as many times as is required. Her salvation lies within the walls of that garden. Her life is in your hands."

Now she sleeps. I pray this remedy will give her at least one night of peace and badly needed rest. I do not know how many hours she has before her illness returns in full force. There is no time to waste. I will enter the poison garden at dawn to face the second task the Poisons have set for me.

I fear this task will be even more difficult than the first, for the moonflower vine outside my window is weeping, and will not tell me why.

17

THE EARLY MORNING IS COLD and dark as Mr. Luxton leads me to the poison garden. We walk in silence except for the jingle of his keys.

Silence for him, at least. I choose not to hear the sobs, the warnings, the cries of fear that accompany our journey. Every blossom, tree, and blade of grass in Northumberland seeks to prevent me from arriving at the very place I am hell-bent on going.

"If Jessamine wakes, do not tell her where I am," I say as Mr. Luxton and I reach the gate. "She would be distressed if she knew I had returned here."

"I doubt she will wake soon. She slept fitfully, and called out during the night." Once more he slips the key into the iron lock. Then he turns to me. "I have come to believe that you possess a kind of genius about these plants, Weed. What I must painstakingly accomplish with years of study, you seem to perceive in a flash—like Isaac Newton and his apple! Be resolute. Learn what you can. I will be waiting."

I step through the gate, and the mist envelops me once more.

"Welcome back, lamb killer." Snakeweed's voice coils around me, and I shiver with disgust.

"Don't be offended, Master Weed; I am sure she means it as a compliment." Dumbcane chuckles. "Your second task may suit you better than the first. Tell him, Larkspur."

That piping voice trills, "Oh, it is a very heroic task. You must defend the weak against the strong. Are you willing?"

"I am."

"Tear off one of my stalks, then, and I will tell you

232

what to do. Choose the one with the prettiest flowers, please! I do so love to be admired. . . ."

I do as the plant tells me, and follow its singsong instructions to walk through the shrouded air. Finally I burst through the silver fog into blinding sunlight. I stand on the footpath that leads to the crossroads, the one that winds like a ribbon through the fields and hills of Hulne Park.

"You have memories of this place, don't you?" Larkspur asks.

I nod. "In happier times, Jessamine and I walked here every day."

"But did you not once see a killing here?" The childlike voice is suddenly harsh. "Did you not once stand by and do nothing? 'The stoat should say grace.' I believe that was all the noble Master Weed had to say on the subject."

I startle at the accusation, but then my cheeks burn with shame. "A stoat killed a rabbit here," I admit. "I remember. At the time I thought only plants could suffer so keenly. Not animals. Not humans. Now I know differently."

"Really? How?"

"Because of the suffering I have seen. And because I am human," I answer in a choked voice. "Because I, too, suffer—when I watch Jessamine in pain—I suffer keenly, too."

"How interesting!" Larkspur's high laugh fills my ear. "I wonder: If such a thing happened again, how would you behave now?"

As if commanded by the tall wand of blue blossoms, a stoat emerges from beneath the hedge. Sniffing and jumpy, it is on the hunt. It skitters and zigzags along the edge of the path in search of its prey.

I see the rabbit before the stoat does. Fat and oblivious, it chews a patch of clover and hunkers low to the ground. The stoat is instantly alert. It crouches, preparing to leap at the back of the rabbit's neck.

It is exactly as it happened before—except this time I am ready. A broken branch I snatch from the ground waits in my hand. Before the stoat can pounce, I strike it hard, once to the back of the head. A single shudder runs through its long body, and then it lies still.

Whether or not the rabbit is grateful I cannot say. It looks at me blinkingly for a moment, then hops away to safety.

"That was heroic, indeed!" Larkspur exclaims. "Did you enjoy it?"

"I did not. But the rabbit lives. Are you satisfied?" Disgusted, I let the bloodied stick drop to the dirt.

"Too bad. I thought you might have enjoyed it, a little. But you must walk a little farther now, ten paces up the path. I have something else to show you, something very dear, and now very sad, too."

Grudgingly I walk ten stride lengths up the path, to a dense growth of forsythia. Beneath the shrub, nestled among leaves of ivy, a litter of newborn stoat kittens lies cuddled in a pulsing, ivory-colored heap.

"Poor mama stoat," Larkspur remarks. "With no mother to nurse them they cannot survive, of course. It will be a slow, pitiful, mewling death, of cold, and hunger, and thirst."

I tremble with fury and frustration. "But was

that not the task you set me? To defend the helpless against the strong?"

"Indeed it was, Master Weed. But who is to say who is helpless, and who is strong?" The strength of the evil child's voice is fading now. "If you seek the power to alter fate, you must also bear responsibility for the consequences. For you cannot change the fate of only one being; all fates are intertwined."

"I performed the task," I protest. "I did what you bid me do."

"You defended the weak from the strong." Larkspur speaks as if from far away. "But who will defend these poor weak infants against you?"

When I return, the Poisons are waiting for me.

"That didn't take long. But I wish to ask you, Master Weed: Why did you not kill the stoat kittens as well?" Snakeweed's voice cuts like a blade. "It would have been a more merciful death than leaving them to starve by the road."

"Heartless Snakeweed! You think killing is the

236

solution to everything. And since when have you cared about being merciful?" Dumbcane's bass voice rumbles the earth beneath my feet. "Well done, lamb-killer Weed. Mighty stoat-killer Weed! Your second task is complete, and your reward awaits. Or, in the heat of all your killing, have you forgotten about saving the life of your sweet Jessamine? She is weak, so weak, poor girl. Not long for your world, I'm afraid."

"Give me the cure." *How I wish I could pull them all up by the roots and tear them to shreds*, I think, and then, *No—that is what they want—to make me think as they do, with no reverence for life, no pity, no mercy—*

Moonseed uncurls a large flat leaf, and presents another bundle of herbs and leaves.

"Will this cure her?" I ask.

"No. Not yet."

"Will it rouse her again, even for a short time?"

"On the contrary—it will plunge her into a deep sleep, almost unto death," Moonseed explains. "Her heart will scarcely beat. No power on earth

237

will be able to wake her. But you must give her this mixture nevertheless, if she is to have any chance of surviving."

The thought of giving Jessamine a medicine that will bring her one step closer to death fills me with dread. "Why must I?" I demand.

"She nears the end of her strength. This will conserve what life is left in her. It will give you more time."

"And you need time." Snakeweed's voice seethes with scorn. "Time to perform your third, and final, task."

"Final it shall be, for I grow weary of your evil games." Bitterly I take the packet of herbs and begin walking in the direction of the gate.

"A word to the wise, Master Weed," Dumbcane calls after me. "Next time you want to kill something, use a little poison. It's so much easier—and less messy—than bashing in heads with a stick."

His laughter increases and grows out of control, until it becomes a rolling, rumbling, sickening sound, like the fall of an avalanche. "Use a little poison, why don't you? Ha ha ha ha ha!"

Mr. Luxton hovers near me as, with trembling hands, I spoon the mixture between Jessamine's lips. As the potion trickles down her throat, she shudders and gasps, as if this would be her last breath. Before our eyes, she sinks into a blue-tinged stillness it would be all too easy to mistake for death.

"Fascinating," Mr. Luxton says, gazing at his daughter's lifeless form. "Does she feel any pain, I wonder? Is she aware of us at all, or has she been sent into some mysterious, twilight sleep, in which she has no knowledge of the passage of time?"

"I hope she feels no pain," I say softly. My heart breaks as I look at her. *Will I ever hear her voice again?* I think. *Will we ever again walk together through the fields and forests?* And her lips—how alive they were, once! How still and cold they are now.

I tuck the blankets snugly around her. Her chest barely rises. The pulse I seek in her wrist is slow and so faint as to be nearly imperceptible. I knew nothing of love before meeting Jessamine, and now I am left to wonder: Is this how it works? A teardrop's worth of happiness dissolved in an ocean of loss?

I would do anything to save her, no matter how base or cruel. I know that now. The Poisons have taught me that. For the love of her, I did the one thing my beloved—my betrothed!—made me swear not to do. And now she lies before me, all but dead.

"You must try again, Weed," Mr. Luxton urges. "You must go back to the garden. You must learn everything you can, so we can save her from this curséd, nameless disease. . . ."

He talks on and on in this insistent way, as he scribbles away in his book of cures. Gazing down at the lifeless mask that now stands in for my dear Jessamine's face, I fear it has all been a mistake. I should never have listened to the Poisons, or gone to them for help.

But now it is too late. I have no choice but to fin-ish what I have started, for I do not know how to rouse her from this trance. Only the Poisons know. Her life may have been in my hands, once. Now it is in theirs.

Welcome back, Jessamine. It was very quiet and lonely here while you were gone. How do you feel now? Rested?

No. I feel very weak, very tired. Everything is slow and strange. I feel as if I am made of lead.

Poor, afflicted child. You are so pale, and so very close to death—see how the light shines through you? My gossamer girl. It is most becoming.

Oleander, are you poisoning me? Is that why I am so ill?

I rule over the Poisons, lovely. I do not administer them.

But I have been sick before in my life, yet this is the first time illness has brought me to your realm. Might that mean that poison is involved?

Clever! Like father, like daughter. I am impressed.

What is wrong with me, then? You must know!

Oh, I do, lovely. I do.

Then why will you not tell me? Or tell Weed, so that he might save me?

It is not my place to say. If you wish, I will take you somewhere where all your questions may find their own answers.

Where?

Someplace far away. Someplace you have always wanted to visit.

Will I be safe there?

As safe as you are anywhere, my sweet . . .

Careful, Weed!

Careful!

Beware . . .

Take care . . .

The warning whispers of the plants follow me everywhere. The flowers sing high, a wail of terror. The hedgerows bark stern orders: *Retreat!* The trees of the forest chant in a deep-throated chorus of foreboding: *beware . . . beware . . . beware . . .*

But I cannot listen. I will not. I slip through the

gate of the poison garden—there is no point in keeping it locked anymore, for evil is everywhere now.

"We were not sure you would return," Dumbcane booms. "We thought that perhaps it had all become too unpleasant. Too compromising."

"Then you misjudge me." My voice is flat with rage. "I have no pride or virtue left to protect. I would trade my life for Jessamine's, if you would accept it. Tell me what I must do to save her, and I will do it."

"How romantic," Snakeweed snaps. "You speak so nobly, Master Weed, but there is nothing noble about what you must do to save your beloved."

"Indeed, the third task is the worst of all," Moonseed says, in his melodious way. "Can you guess what it is?"

"Yes, guess!" Larkspur cries. "A guessing game; that will be amusing!"

Is there no end to their toying with me? I swallow my rage and reply. "The first two tasks resulted in death. Death wrought by inaction, and death wrought by wrongheaded justice. I know the third task will

243

bring death as well—and you say it is the worst of all." My voice is hollow, as if it comes from someplace far away. "The worst death of all—is the slaughter of the innocent."

"He is clever, so very clever!" Larkspur quivers with delight. "I think he is as clever as our prince—"

"Hush, child," Snakeweed snarls, and then addresses me. "Well done, Master Weed. You must slaughter the innocent. For if you dare demand the power to cure, you must also embrace the power to kill. That is the lesson of the poison garden."

"You are mad to bid me do this!" My temper is unleashed now, and I have no control of my words. "If there is one thing I have learned, from loving Jessamine and even from the evil tasks you have made me do, it is that all forms of life are worthy of compassion. There is no life without death, true, but needless killing is an abomination."

One of Dumbcane's thick, broad leaves falls and drifts to the ground. "Stand at the crossroads. Slaughter the innocent. Only then can your beloved be saved. So commands the Prince of Poisons."

My breath comes fast, my heart pounds. I reach down to pick up the leaf, and in doing so I know I am beaten.

"Who is this prince?" I ask in defeat. "Is he the one I have done so much evil to please?"

"You need not ask who he is," Snakeweed croons. "If you earn his regard, he will reveal himself."

This time I take Dumbcane's advice. My murder weapon is in a small vial in my pocket, a lethal tincture of leaves from the poison garden mixed with a small amount of whiskey I steal from Mr. Luxton's cabinet.

I stand at the crossroads as I have been told to do. People go by, farmers, merchants, women and children, beggars and pilgrims. They are on their way to the sea, to market, to Alnwick.

Who among them will be my victim? Is it truly up to me to choose?

If only I could *choose.* I think of all the persecutors

245

I have known in my life. Not only Tobias Pratt, but so many others who reviled me as a witch, a freak, an outcast. *If one of them would walk by, perhaps I could bring myself to kill,* I think. *But they would hardly be innocent.*

The parade of humanity passes, singly, in twos and threes. I watch, and wait. And mourn, for what I must now do to save Jessamine's life makes me unworthy of her love. Whether she lives or dies, I know I have lost her.

I have lost her, forever.

Accepting the bitterness of that truth steels me against all compassion. My newly opened heart slams shut with an iron clang, and is sealed with a lock that has no key. Once more I am cold and unfeeling, as bloodless as the plants I have preferred to humans all my life.

Now, at last, I am ready to kill.

Soon a man in a long dark coat and odd hat approaches; when he reaches the crossing he pauses and addresses me. "Repent, friend," he warns. "The heavens are filled with omens, and sin runs rampant on the earth."

The sun disappears, blotted out by the dark wings of a raven that circles overhead.

"Repent," the preacher says again, with a nervous glance upward. "Repent, for the end is near."

"Nearer than you know," I reply. I tackle him to the ground and drag him behind the hedge where we cannot be seen from the road.

"Do not rob me, sir! I have nothing—repent! Repent!" His ceaseless chatter makes it easy to slip the poison between his lips. He gags, then swallows, and looks at me, aghast, confused. Then the convulsions begin.

I close my eyes and pin him to the ground as the life thrashes out of his body. I hold fast, and soon the flesh beneath my hands is soft, yielding, springy as wool.

I feel the gorge rise in my throat. As I was once sickened at the thought of eating a carrot, now I am revulsed by taking a human life. I think of Jessamine—

how glad she would be to know that, and how much she would hate me if she knew what I have done.

Forgive me, my beloved, I am doing this for you—

I look down. It is no preacher at all. It is a young ewe that I imprison in my murderous hands, plump and covered with fleece.

Have I gone mad? I close my eyes, then look again. It is the preacher, eyes bulging, wordlessly begging for mercy.

"What is it that I kill?" I cry in despair.

Does it matter? The answer comes back, soothing, seductive, reasonable beyond measure. *Death is death. If your victim lives, Jessamine dies. If it dies, she lives. Since all lives are of equal value, what difference does it make which one you save?*

KRAAAAAAAAAAAAAH!

A raw, cruel cry fills the air—is it me who screams? Or the raven?

I release my prey and stand. The convulsions have stopped, but the preacher is not yet dead. He pants and flops about on the ground, helpless as a fish as the

248

paralysis spreads through his body, and stares at me, wild-eyed with fear.

It must end. I have no weapon save my hands. I could beg a branch from a tree and fashion a club from it, or a sharp stake, but I will make no other living thing party to this wretched deed. I find a heavy stone, sharp edged. I do not even bother to hide it, for I know my victim can neither fight nor flee.

I raise the stone above my head.

The ewe gazes up at me with its trusting brown eyes. It gives a soft bleat of welcome.

"No!" screams the preacher. "Spare me, friend—God forgive you—"

"Thank you for what I am about to receive," I gasp, and strike the death blow.

18

We have arrived. Listen carefully, my lovely: Can you hear?

Shrieking. Moaning. All I hear is suffering. What is this place? It is like a museum of death!

Not a museum. Think of it as a laboratory.

Is it yours?

No. Only a person who thirsted to know—who insisted on knowing, no matter the cost—would create a place such as this.

You mean, a person like my father?

There's an interesting notion. Your father knows a

great deal about plants. So does your beloved Crabgrass, come to think of it. Why, if I were you I would be very suspicious of both of them! People like that are prone to do anything to get the knowledge they crave.

I don't understand—

Look around you. If one wished to determine, for example, how much strychnine it would take to kill a grown man—or how many hours a generous dose of hemlock would take to paralyze, but not kill, the victim— there really is only one way to find out.

Where are we, Oleander? Who are these people?

You need not concern yourself with who they are; no one else does. A madhouse is a very convenient place to find people whom no one will miss. And the madhouses in London are overflowing! The city alone is enough to drive a man out of his wits.

Then—we are in London?

Why the stricken face, Jessamine? You always wanted to visit London, did you not?

I thought Father might take me someday—he goes there—often, he goes there—he does not tell me what he *does there, though. Oh, I do not like this! Is this what you wish me to think? That my father experiments on madmen to learn about the poisons he grows?*

He is a clever man. And that would be a clever plan.

It would be murder!

Life and death, death and life, is that all you flesh bodies can think of? Look at the plants: We die back to the ground every winter. We wither and fade; our leaves turn to ash and blow away. And yet you do not hear us complain. Happily we return to the earth and die our little, temporary death, for we know we will come back, one way or another.

That is because you do not die like we do. For you death is not even real.

Death is real, make no mistake. But it is also an illusion. An interesting paradox, is it not? Why do you weep, my lovely?

My father—a murderer, a poisoner!—surely it cannot be true—

If you did not think it were true, you would not be weeping. Another interesting paradox! But cry, cry as much as you like—we have to fly again, back the way we came, but we will travel faster now, for time is running out—and there is one more thing you must see—

Here we are. Unfortunate creature. Open your eyes now, Jessamine: do you see? The resemblance is striking; she looks just like you. Poor girl, she must be in agony. See how she screams and screams, and begs for her suffering to be over—have all your questions been answered yet?

Oleander, tell me the truth—who is she?

The truth? I fear that is unwise, but if you insist: She is you, my dear. You seem to have taken a turn for the worse. That dimwitted fiancé of yours is certainly in no rush to cure you of whatever it is that ails you.

Stop this! I cannot bear it anymore, please—

You see why it is better to leave the frail flesh body behind? Imagine being trapped inside all of—that. The mess, the noise. The pain! Truly, you are much better off here, with me. Stay with me, Jessamine. Stay . . . no answer? You are considering my offer, though, I can see how it tempts you—I hear it in the terrified flutter of your heart, fast as a bird's—

From the look of it I will soon be dead. You will have to find another companion.

Perhaps I will, or perhaps you will change your mind—oh, dear; it appears your incompetent caretakers have found some new, vile potion to force down your throat. Come away now, this is not something you ought to watch . . . it is much, much too upsetting. . . .

I STAGGER BACK TO THE GARDEN, sticky with blood.

"Dumbcane? Snakeweed? I have returned."

There is silence. I sense only the chilling silver mist, enwrapping me in its tendrils.

"Moonseed? Larkspur? Speak, Poisons! I have performed the tasks you asked of me. Now you must give me the cure I seek." I shout in anger to keep myself from weeping, for I know my soul is lost. I have killed, and killed, and killed again, and there is no amount of grace that can save me now.

"My subjects—the ones you call the Poisons—are not here."

A young man rises from the earth. Some might

call him beautiful. His hair is silver as wormwood, his lips are stained red as a yew berry. Twinned dark shapes—can they be wings?—lie folded against his back. He approaches me with outstretched arms.

"Welcome home, Weed," he says.

I am exhausted with games and trickery, and murder still flows in my veins. It takes all my strength not to strike out at this smug creature and let his own crimson blood dye the earth beneath our feet.

"Who are you?" I hiss in fury.

The dark shapes on his back rise and flex. They are enormous wings made of dark, leathery leaves, stretched over a skeleton of branches that are gnarled and forked as a witch hazel tree. Only now does he lift his eyes to mine. They are wide and vividly green, like my own.

"Don't you know me, Weed? We have met before, more than once. Surely you remember—the first time was long ago. . . ."

The hypnotic power of his voice is impossible to resist. I close my eyes. My nostrils fill with the tang of salt air.

"I remember," I say, dazed, as the long-forgotten images wash over me. "When I was a boy I used to run off; one time I made it to the docks and stowed away on a trading vessel bound for the Low Countries. A fortnight into the voyage, the ship was boarded by pirates. The crew bargained for their freedom. They offered to hand me over as a slave. I was terrified. I prayed for some way to defend myself."

"And your prayers were answered. Remember?"

The horrors of the past flood my senses: *The sudden, violent illness that swept over our captors but left us untouched, the vomiting, the stench of decay, the bodies thrown overboard one by one as the pirates died in agony . . .*

"Our attackers grew sick and weak," I answer in a daze. "Their numbers dwindled, and soon we were able to defeat them."

"There is more, Weed. Remember?" His sinuous voice lures the memories from my mind. "The pirates were starving; they had been sailing for weeks with no provisions left but hardtack and whiskey. After seizing your vessel, they bound the crew in ropes. They took you for the ship's boy, and ordered you to the galley to prepare a meal."

"I remember," I whisper hoarsely.

"You made a stew, and seasoned it with rare spices from the hold of the ship—the same precious cargo they had hoped to steal. It was I who guided your hand that day."

"It seems my thanks is overdue." I bow my head, more in shame than in gratitude.

"You are most welcome. And now that your memory has been rekindled, do you recall my name as well?"

I close my eyes once more and conjure the smell of the sea. "Oleander," I whisper. "I remember now. But I called you Angel—because of the wings."

"And I called you Weed." His wings spread and arch upward. "Poor, straggly Weed. Because no one ever wanted you, no matter where you went or how many seeming 'miracles' you performed. How was I to know the name would stick?"

257

"Will you come to my aid again now?" My heart twists with a last, agonizing surge of hope. "I seek a cure for Jessamine Luxton. I have done all that was asked of me in exchange for it. Time is short—I beg of you—"

He ignores my pleading. He looks up at me, and I am again startled by the emerald color of his eyes, so similar to my own. "Poor Jessamine," he murmurs. "She was truly quite lovely."

"What do you mean?" I cry, stepping toward him. "Is it already too late?"

"Not yet. Not quite. Foolish, brave girl! She is so near death, on the precipice, really. And oh, how she suffers! Unlike your many victims, Jessamine still bears the full burden of life in the flesh. It is terrible, terrible. Most people would rather die than endure what she now endures."

"Give me the cure," I say thickly. "Please."

"There is something we need to discuss first." His wings rise and flex again, chilling me with their shadow. "Time and again you have entered my realm to bargain for a cure for your beloved. You have demanded it, begged for it, you have even killed for it. But you have never bothered to ask: What is it, exactly, that ails your sweet Jessamine?"

"To save her is all that matters to me."

"But aren't you the least bit curious? Is it the dropsy? The ague? A rare intestinal parasite, perhaps?"

"Enough!" It is all I can do to keep from throttling him. "She is near death, you said so yourself. There is no time left for talk—"

"I find your lack of curiosity . . . curious, that is all. Almost as if you would prefer not to know." He looks at me intently. "Humor me. Ask me what ails her."

This is a trick, I can feel it, yet once again I have no choice but to play along. "What ails her?" My voice is hollow.

"She is being poisoned."

"It is impossible," I retort, but fear plummets through my body like a stone. "I have scarcely left her side. No one has been to the cottage. No food or drink has passed her lips except what I have fed her myself."

"That's just it, my dear Weed. Those vile potions you keep dribbling through her tender, kissable lips— *blech!* Enough poison in there to paralyze a cow."

"That medicine was prepared by her father! No one else has been near her." But already my hands begin to clench with rage—*it cannot be*—

Oleander's powerful wings beat in a slow, accusing rhythm. "Think, Weed! Did you never wonder what truly happened that night, the night you and your bride-to-be went half mad with passion and entered her father's study to taste the forbidden fruit, as it were? Did you not suspect for one moment that there were forces more powerful than your simpering calf love at work? That, perhaps, there might have been something in the tea that Jessamine's beloved father so carefully prepared for you both before he left for London?"

"How do you know this?"

Oleander's eyes flash as if they would burst into flame. His voice soars with rage. "I know because it was here he came—without my permission!—to my realm, knife in hand, to shear the tender growth from my loyal subjects and mix their very limbs into an elixir of love that would inflame the blood and erase inhibition! A few sips would all but guarantee that you, you callow, ardent misfit, and that perfectly ripe, lovestruck girl would lose all reason, abandon all restraint—"

"Curb your tongue, evil prince!"

"Evil? I am nearly a saint compared to that clever, wicked Thomas Luxton! He witnessed the spark of affection between you; all he had to do was nurture it into a mighty, consuming flame." Oleander spreads his great wings fully, until they blot out half the sky. "That you and his quivering, untouched daughter performed so *lavishly*, even providing him with grounds for a betrothal—why, it must have been more than any proud father could have hoped for! Now you were bound together, in life and in death. Now he could ask anything of you, for her sake, and you, righteous prig that you are, would jump to comply."

"But to what end would he do this?" I cry. "For what purpose?"

"For what purpose, you ask. How appropriate."

261

With a powerful thrust of his wings he rises into the air. "You flesh bodies are so obsessed with goodness, yet no other form of life on earth is capable of such cruelty. You need only convince yourselves your transgressions serve some 'purpose.' Even if it is only greed, or lust, or the raw desire for power that drives you. You will spill the blood of your kinsmen, lay waste to the earth itself, wreak havoc, and cause unspeakable suffering—any and all sins are justified, as long as they are a means to your precious, righteous 'purpose.'"

His voice pierces me through. The icy wind from his beating wings freezes my blood.

"So it has been with you, Master Weed. You would do anything if you thought it might save Jessamine; in that, you have proven yourself human to the core. And so it is with Luxton. Once he fixed on his 'purpose,' the rest of his misdeeds followed with barely a moment of remorse: First, a venomous toast—"

The earth shifts beneath me. "The absinthe—" I stammer. "The toast for our engagement—the sugar cube—"

"You see how carefully the trap was laid? For, unless you were willing to die for your precious fiancée, you would never have dared come here, to my intoxicating garden of death. Luxton made you willing to kill, even willing to die—all in exchange for a few measly recipes."

"Recipes?"

"Of course." His laughter is like a rain of daggers. "Without your heroic efforts, Master Weed, all those pages in the apothecary's precious book of poisons would still be blank."

Now in flight, he swoops and circles me like a vulture. "How shocked you look!" he crows. "How horrified! That a man would poison his own daughter to gain power, in the form of a little deadly but exquisitely valuable knowledge—does this surprise you, Weed? Even after all my Poisons have taught you? Haven't you been paying attention at all?"

He swoops down once more. The tip of his finger, sharp as a thorn, draws itself gently across my cheek. It is no more than the touch of a breeze, but I feel the hot blood well up and drip to the corner of my mouth, until the sharp metal taste is on my tongue.

Now rage fills me, the bile rises. I am poisoned, finally, with my own blood and anger, and there will be no cure for me but killing Thomas Luxton—not with a coward's secret poisons, but with my own avenging hands—

Speechless with fury, I turn and sprint back to the cottage.

"Off you go, then, Master Weed! Consider it your fourth task." Oleander's laughter carries on the wind. "Vengeance against the wicked!"

I feel everything now, Oleander. Every moment is agony. Please—make it stop—

It is what you wished for, lovely. Remember?

I only wished to live. Not to die. And not to stay—oh, have mercy!—not to be trapped eternally in this poisoned half-life, with you—

You can still change your mind. My lips are sweet as the juice of the belladonna berry; one kiss and you will

264

be in bliss, and stay in bliss, forevermore. As will I. How glorious it would be, if only you would let me relieve your suffering and anoint you with pleasure instead. My poison princess; that is what you could be—

You said you would give Weed the cure for me. Did you?

I said I would, and unlike some people, I never break my promises.

You told him I was dying?

Of course, lovely. I told him everything. He knows what ails you, and how to save you.

Then where is he?

Hmm. I am not sure. Perhaps he had something more important to attend to. . . .

Oh, I cannot bear it, the pain is too much—I am run through with blades still glowing from the forge, truly these are the fires of hell—Weed!

19

Panting like a dog, I search the cottage, the gardens, the sheep meadows. Guided by the whispers of the grass, and the pointing branches of the trees, I finally find Luxton in the stone circle that marks the ruins of the ancient hospital. He crouches on the ground, satchel slung across his body, running his fingers through the earth. Despite the warm weather, he wears gloves.

How fitting it is to confront his evil deeds here, in this ancient cesspit of tainted blood and amputated limbs!

At my arrival he stands, his back to me. A tiny

seedling dangles from his gloved fingers. "Monkshood," he murmurs. "A few leaves on the skin cause tingling and numbness. When ingested, a tiny dose lessens pain, a larger dose slows the heartbeat and respiration, slower and slower, until . . . well, I am sure you already know." He looks at me with an arched eyebrow. "After all, you know everything. Don't you, Weed? But only when it is too late, it seems."

"You are the cause of Jessamine's illness," I spit out. "You have been poisoning her."

Moving slowly and calmly, he tucks the seedling into his satchel and brushes the dirt off his hands. "Who told you that, Weed? The rhododendron? The daffodils?" He waves some sheets of paper. "Yes, I could not resist knowing. I read your garden journal. How foolish of you to confess your secret there, where anyone at all could see. I took the liberty of removing those pages—for your own protection, and, as it turns out, for my own."

I cannot speak—it is too late to deny the truth— shall I just kill him to silence him? What is one more killing, once the first is done?

"How I long to know how you do it, Weed," he says, tucking the pages back into his satchel. "To communicate with plants directly! It is unimaginable, yet I have seen the proof of it. What a shame there is no time for us to talk; there are so many questions I want to ask you. Yet there is only one question worth asking now: Do you wish to kill Jessamine? Or save her?"

"You are the one who kills her!" I cry. "I wish to save her—from you."

"If I intended to kill her she would be dead." He takes a step toward me. "And what I have done, I have done for good, nay, excellent, reasons. Reasons that a creature—or, let us be frank, a monster—with your powers could never understand."

"If I am a monster, then you are surely a demon—"

"I am her father, and I have dominion over her!" His eyes burn. "You wish to destroy me, I can see that. But I wonder: Will the brief thrill of vengeance be worth the cost? An hour ago Jessamine was still alive, though barely. If you want her to die, there is no better way to guarantee it than to kill me right now."

"Killing you kills the man who has poisoned her," I exclaim. "That you are also her father erases all hope of mercy. Make your peace with whatever God you dare believe in, Luxton. You are a dead man."

I lunge for his throat, but he evades me.

"But what of you, my self-appointed executioner?" he taunts. "Kill me and you will surely hang on the gallows."

"Not when I tell them what you have done."

"Who will believe you? Not anyone whom I ever healed, and that is half the county. Not the duke, or the duke's followers. Not Jessamine—especially not Jessamine! My darling, innocent girl. She knows little of the evils of this world; I have made sure of that." Confident, he takes a step closer. "No, Weed. You will die by the noose, and the hatred of the woman you love will bear you to your murderer's unhallowed grave."

"Do you think I care what happens to me?" I reply. "I was ready to die for her before, and remain so. Your words do not move me."

269

"Then perhaps this will: When you and I are both dead, what becomes of Jessamine? Who will care for her? Put your rage aside and think of her for a change. Her frail heart will shatter. Would you have her blood on your hands, in addition to the friar, and whomever else you have killed in your time?"

"You are wrong about the friar—" I cry, but I stop. Does it even matter? For I have surely killed—what right have I to Jessamine's love, now?

His eyes glitter with ambition. "What knowledge you must possess! To poison at will, to kill and leave no trace. If you could only put aside your righteous, stubborn anger, Weed! I know men who would pay any price for this knowledge. Together we could have such power, such riches—"

His words are worse than poison—I can bear no more. "Murderer! Poisoner! Your own daughter is near death because of you! Do you imagine that your deeds can go unpunished? I will not listen to you argue for another second—"

I seize him and knock him to the ground. My hands

270

encircle his throat, ready to silence him for good. His life is mine to take, all I have to do is squeeze—

"There is a way to save her," he croaks in desperation. "I will leave England and never return. You stay and care for Jessamine. Tell her whatever fiction you like about my departure. Or tell her the truth, if you are that selfish and cruel. But if you love her at all, you will carry the burden of what you know alone."

Now which of us is the monster? I think as my fingers tighten. Even with my hands wrapped around his throat, he counsels deceit and plans his escape—

"I would leave my home and my daughter behind forever, in order that Jessamine may live in peace," he gasps. "But it seems you would rather take vengeance than do what is best for her. It's plain—which one of us—loves her more—"

Now he can no longer speak. His eyes start to bulge and roll upward. Rage shrinks the edges of my vision. All I can see is his lips, moving uselessly like those of a fish flopping in its death throes on the dock, desperate for a last, lifesaving swallow of air.

271

KRAAAAAAAAAAH!

The cruelest sound in the world stabs through me, forces me back, loosens my grip. Now freed, Luxton rolls to his side, gasping as the raw breath sears his lungs.

"Weed!" Oleander's winged form erases all light as it hovers above us. "Forgive me for interrupting this charming scene, but surely you have forgotten something important?"

"Leave me, evil prince!" I bellow at the heavens.

"If you wish me to leave, I will—but I believe your beloved Jessamine will be needing this. If she is to live, that is."

I gaze up and look more closely. A bundle of herbs and roots dangles from his fingers.

"It is an antidote to the dreadful brew her father has been using to poison her. He thinks himself clever, too clever to kill a girl by accident—but he is, as they say, only human. He overestimated her strength. He has made her too ill to recover, even if the poisoning stops. Without this cure, she has less than a quarter-hour to live."

He rises, and the bundle flies out of my reach.

"Give it to me!"

"Only if you let Luxton go."

"He deserves to die!"

"So do we all, I'm afraid. Yet some of us live on, and on, and on—"

Luxton watches me, transfixed. "Who are you talking to?" he whispers in hoarse amazement. I ignore the wretch, for Oleander still dangles the antidote just out of my reach.

"Fine. I will let him go," I say desperately. "He is free! Look, I have released him; he can go where he will. The farther away, the better. Now—please—"

"You misunderstand me, Weed. Luxton must stay here and care for Jessamine, of course. And you must leave, now, and never return."

"What! Why should I be the one to leave?" This final cruelty is too much for me. My knees buckle and pitch me to the earth.

"You know why. You are lost, Weed. A killer, a monster. You are no longer fit to be a husband for

273

Jessamine Luxton, if you ever were—and what else could you be? You love her too much to be a servant, or a friend—"

"But she loves me, too," I insist.

"She loved you before. But now? Now there is blood on your hands, Weed. She deserves better, so much better, than you—if you truly loved her you would see that."

The antidote bobs in the air.

I am trapped. Oleander has plunged me into the very pit of evil, where there is no power to do right. And yet I must do something. I am at the crossroads again, but the four directions lead to ruin, misery, loneliness, death—

"All right!" I cry, my heart breaking even as I say it. "I will go. I will leave."

With a graceful swerve, Oleander drops the antidote into my outstretched hands. He rises up above us then, and circles higher and higher, until the black speck of evil disappears into the hellfire of the sun.

Luxton stares at me, and past me. His eyes scan the sky, but he sees nothing. He looks even more terrified

274

than when I had my hands on his throat.

"Give her this mixture at once; make haste!" I shove the antidote roughly at his chest. "It is the cure to your filthy poisons. Give it to your daughter now, or you will surely die. And beware, Luxton," I add, my voice dripping with menace. "There is nowhere on this green earth you can go but where I will have news of your evildoing. Every patch of moss, every blade of grass, every weed that grows in the stone walls of your home is my spy and ally. If you ever harm one hair on Jessamine's head again, you will die a death more horrible than even your wildest nightmares could imagine."

Time is wasting, Weed—

"Go!" I scream it to the heavens. "Go now, for the next time I lay eyes on you, I swear, it will be to kill you."

I give Luxton a violent push. Even as he coughs and gags, he climbs to his feet. His eyes fly up in terror, but he cannot see Oleander. Where the Prince of Poisons was, there is only an absence, a place with neither light nor shadow. It is a kind of emptiness that has not existed since before the world began.

With scarcely a backward glance, Luxton makes his way to the path and half stumbles, half runs back to the ancient ruins of his home. The antidote is still clutched tightly in his hands. I watch until he disappears over the crest of the hill.

Live, Jessamine. I will it, with every drop of strength I possess. *Live, and remember me. I will never be far, and my friends—the flowers, the trees, the tender vine that curls around your window and guards you while you sleep—they will always be watching. And so will I.*

As I stand, awash in rage and despair, a low, sad rumble from the distant forest offers me a refuge. I will go, for I too must live. My life's purpose now is to watch, and protect. And, if need be, to avenge.

I step onto the path and turn my back to Hulne Park, to the cottage, to Jessamine—to the only happiness I have ever known.

Luxton's satchel lies in the dirt before me. I lift it. I can tell by the weight and shape of it what it contains: his book of cures. Thomas Luxton's poison diary. Filled with the information I gave him, purchased nearly at the price of his daughter's life.

It was his most precious possession.

Now it is mine.

Alas, my Jessamine; we do not have much time left.

What does that mean, Oleander? Does it mean I will die?

I don't want you to leave me, Jessamine. There is so much I have yet to tell you.

You have already told more than I can bear.

We have hardly begun. The truth of things is so cruel, so beautiful—so much more thrilling than you can imagine. Stay with me. I will reveal dark secrets you never dreamed existed. We will fly everywhere you ever longed to see. Stay. You will not be sorry.

What secrets? Oleander—I cannot see you anymore—the silver mist turns to darkness—is it the end? Oh, I am afraid! Perhaps you are right, perhaps I should stay—for my father is a murderer, and Weed has abandoned me—why should I return to them? And you,

Oleander—cruel and strange as you are—you have told me only the truth . . . you have tried to help me, I see that now. . . . Oleander, I reach for you, where are you? I clutch something in the darkness, but it is only a leaf come loose in my hand—

Too late, I am afraid. Good-bye for now, lovely lady. When you are ready to meet again, come to the poison garden. . . . I am always there. . . . I will be waiting. . . .

My eyes open. Curtains flutter in the breeze, and bright yellow sunshine floods in my bedchamber window. The light stings. Tears form, blinding me again. But not before I see Father's face hovering above me.

He looks like an old man. A frightened, evil old man.

And Weed is nowhere to be found.

I feel my leaden body, shackled to the bed by gravity and mortality. I ache everywhere. The sheets are damp with my sweat. My joints ache, my belly is full of pain, my head throbs.

I am alive.

278

Turn the page for a tantalizing peek
at the next Poison Diaries novel,

THE POISON DIARIES:
NIGHTSHADE

"What is it, Jessamine? You look unwell. Let me pre-pare a tonic for you."

I am faint, but I will not admit that to Father. He pours something for me to drink and brings it to me. The glass hovers in front of me. In its swirl of liquid I see visions: *A dying lamb. The madhouses of London. A pair of large, terrifying wings.*

I push the glass away. "I had terrible dreams when I was ill, Father," I say in a low voice. "Some of them were about you. About what you did on your trips to London."

His eyes glitter in the firelight. "Take a sip, my dear. It will steady you."

"I dreamed that you went to the madhouse there. That you fed poison to the lunatics, in order to test your formulas."

He stands so quickly the drink spills. "How strange. The fantasies our minds concoct when we are sick. . . ."

I rise to my feet, clawing at my head as if I could tear that voice out by its roots. "A fantasy? I thought so, too. Now I am not so sure."

Careful, lovely . . . your father has a dreadful temper, you know. . . .

I watch the blue vein on his forehead throb. His words are calm, but his voice is a tightened sinew of rage. "Jessamine, it seems your mind is more affected by your illness than I first supposed. I suggest you go to bed. I know some cures that can help you."

"Your cures!" I practically spit with contempt. "I think your cures are poison, Father. I think everything you have told me is a lie, and that which I believed to

2

be a dream is all too real."

The images take form again—me, flying high over the fields of Northumberland, born aloft by a pair of dark wings. "And Weed's love for me, and mine for him, is the realest thing of all," I gasp. "If you will not tell me where he is, then I will have to look for him myself."

"Enough." Three strides, and he is across the room. "I will tell you what you wish to know. But I warn you, you may regret it." He gestures for me to sit down. "During your illness, Weed became distraught. Because of his extraordinary talent for healing, I believe he felt responsible for curing you, and was driven mad with frustration when he could not. He grew agitated, unreasonable. Finally he left. I could not chase after him, for I did not dare leave your side. You were at death's very threshold that night."

The light of the fire glows behind my father, casting lurid shadows along the stone floor. "He abandoned you, Jessamine, and you should despise him for it, not pine for his return. But you are right to call me a liar: He did not simply run off, as I have told you in the past."

I sit there, unmoving as a statue in church, as Father's voice drops deep. "You were so weak. I thought it would kill you to know the truth. As time passed and you regained your strength, I dared hope you would make your peace with my story and would never have to know the fate of that that coward Weed. I prayed you would forget about him. He fooled us both, for a time. I do not blame you for being deceived by him. I was deceived as well."

The flames leap, and the shadows do their mocking dance. My father's words toll like a bell.

"Weed is dead. He hung himself, in a remote part of the woods of Hulne Park. I found the body myself. The fool!"

Father approaches me and places a hand on my shoulder. I allow myself to soften, to weep. It is not difficult. I shed tears at will these days.

"I thought it would be too cruel to tell you the truth. But it is crueler still to let you go on longing for something that can never be." He steps back and spreads his arms, as if waiting for me to step into his embrace. "I hope you can forgive me, Jessamine. Oh, the curse of being a parent! The sins we commit to ease our children's suffering!"

I rise from the chair. Father takes a step toward me. I wheel from his open arms and race outside, into the storm.

"Jessamine—" His voice follows me to the door, but the moment I am outside the shrieking wind drowns out every sound but the pounding of my own heart. Let Father run after me if he dares. I am one with the storm now, wild and furious, a howl of rage.

"Weed!" I hurl my desperate cry to the starless sky. Up the twisting path I climb. The ground is muck beneath my feet. Am I truly mad, then? I must be, to think the poison garden is the only place left for me to turn.

But how else will I finally discover what is real? How else will I know what is true, and what is a lie?

And when the worst has already happened, what is left to fear?

Unless the worst is yet to come. The thought stops me short. I pause for breath. Eyes closed, I feel the earth spin drunkenly beneath my feet, slipped off its axis like a wheel on a broken axle.

Foolish Jessamine . . . did you really think I was only a dream?

Thunder cracks, loud as a gunshot. I press my hand to my chest. My heart flutters like a trapped bird within the cage of my bones. My hair hangs sodden, like seaweed trailing from the ropes of a sailing ship. My dress is as wet as if I had risen up from the German Ocean and walked ashore.

"Help me," I cry with all the ragged breath I have left. "If you are here, show yourself, I beg you. For I do not know what to believe anymore."

I will show you.

Once more, lightning slashes crookedly across the sky, briefly revealing the path before the world plunges into darkness again. The wind howls and blows, not

6

east to west, but in strange circles that seem as if they would pluck the trees straight up from the ground and hurl them down again like broken toys.

The black gate of the poison garden looms before me. I hurl myself at the unyielding bars. The lock taunts me, an iron apple dangling from a lifeless tree. Exhausted, I collapse to the ground.

I assure you, I am no dream, lovely. I have powers you cannot imagine. I can help you find what you seek. All you need do is ask.

Help me, my heart begs, yet I dare not speak the name of the one to whom I plead. The horrors of my nightmares come back to me ten times over: the torment. The lunatic asylum. My father's wickedness and murderous lies.

Nothing about this world is what I thought it was. I am lost, and have only one refuge.

"Oleander!" I cry, but the wind swallows all sound. I lift myself from the mud and seize the bars of the gate in my two hands. The wet metal is cold and rough against my cheek. "Please! I need you. I need you to

7

show me the truth . . . as you did once before. . . ."

The sound of the storm changes. To each side of me rain pours, lighting cracks, wind howls. Somehow I am shielded.

I throw my head back and search the sky. Directly above me the night takes form. It is darkness upon darkness, like ink spilled upon black velvet.

The inky stain is in the shape of outspread wings.

For months I have waited for you to come back to me, the Prince of Poisons croons. *And now you are here.*

"Tell me, please," I gasp. The shadow wings beat once, twice. "Is Weed dead or alive?"

Your beloved Crabgrass is rather unkempt at the moment. In a foul temper, and in urgent need of a bath. But yes; he is alive.

The relief I feel is mixed with the sure, sickening knowledge that my father is no more than a murderous villain.

"I must find him—does my father know where he is?"

If your father knew where to find Weed, he would

8

have had him killed by now. He cannot harness Weed's gifts for his own purposes, and he will not have him be a potential rival.

"He is a monster! Oleander, can you help me find Weed?"

I can if I choose to. But first you must prove yourself worthy.

"Tell me what to do."

I want you to avenge your mother's death. Bring justice to her killer. Then you will have earned my aid.

My heart clenches. "My mother was murdered? By whom?"

Who do you think, lovely?

His laughter falls like a rain of ice. *There is no end to the wickedness of humans, is there? It surprises even me, sometimes. When your task is done, then I will help you find what you seek. And you will help me in exchange, when the time comes. For you and I need each other, as you will someday learn. . . .*

"What do you mean?" I cry, but the shadow being ascends to the vault of the night, and is gone.

The rain pours down with doubled fury. I slip and stumble along the muddy path, back to the cottage, too shocked to even weep.

My whole life has been based on lies. And the only being that can help me find Weed is an incarnation of evil itself.

Have I made a terrible mistake in rousing the dark prince? It does not matter, for I must find Weed again, whatever the price.

And this too I swear: No corrupt magistrate, no dim-witted committee of farmers, will stand in judgment of my mother's killer.

No. I will deal with him—with Father—myself.

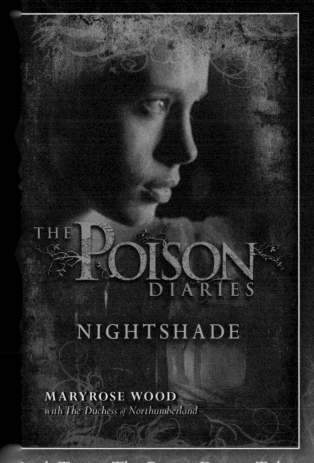